Nightmusic Tina

BY THE SAME AUTHOR

Footprints In The Water

Kittyland

Sure, It Could Happen...

The Elephants' Graveyard

Company of Friends (Play)

Nightmusic

BY THE SAME AUTHOR

Footprints In The Water

Kittyland

Sure, It Could Happen...

The Elephants' Graveyard

Company of Friends (Play)

DECLAN VARLEY

NIGHTMUSIC

Nightmusic _____

Published by Declan Varley

First published in Ireland by

Declan Varley 2000

Copyright (c) Declan Varley 2000

The author asserts the moral right
to be identified as the author of this book

ISBN 0-9539450-0-6

This novel is entirely a work of fiction. The names, characters and incidents portrayed in it are the work of the author's imagination. Any resemblance to actual persons, living or dead, events or localities is entirely coincidental

Set in Optima

Cover illustration by Pat Tracey
Layout by Alison Dickson-Brophy
Proofread by Darina Molloy & Bernadette Prendergast

Printed and bound in Ireland by
Turner Print Group, Longford.

All rights reserved. No part of this publication may be reproduced, stored in a retrieval system, or transmitted in any form or by any means, electronic, mechanical, photocopying, recording or otherwise, without the prior permission of the publishers.

This book is sold subject to the condition that it shall not, by way of trade or otherwise, be lent, re-sold, hired out or otherwise circulated without the publisher's prior consent in any form of binding or cover other than that in which it is published and without a similar condition including this condition being imposed on the subsequent purchaser.

Nightmusic

For Bernadette
who supports all my crazy ventures

Nightmusic

'The only thing worse than a flute is two flutes'

Wolfgang Amadeus Mozart

Nightmusic

The drums and the screams beat out across the summer city.
Rat-a-tat-tat, Rat-a-tat-tat,Rat-a-tat-tat,Rat-a-tat-tat. Even from Salthill, he could make out the distant thuds of the busker's drums. He sat there on Gentian Hill and looked out over Galway Bay and imagined what it would have been like to have been here a thousand years before. Or two thousand even.
And hear other drums beat a similar rhythm.
Marking a sacrifice to the Gods for the good things that had come their way.
And so it must continue.
The drums beat on, the fun lives on and somebody somewhere has to pay for the privilege of living in the fastest growing city in Europe.

*****

Nightmusic

Noel Fogarty flapped at the fan. It didn't stir.
He got up again, rolled up a copy of the *Advertiser* and hit the blades again and this time it went around for a minute and then stopped. The third time, he hit it a right slap, sending the blades around like a chopper and clipping the top of the paper, sending a shower of chopped up *Advertiser* falling gracefully all over the Communications Room.
He stood under and let the breeze blow down on him, making his shirt flap and he uttered a low orgasmic 'oh yeah' to himself. In the background, there was nothing to be heard but the humming of the big console of lights and switches all flickering away, not ringing or anything, just signalling that each walkie talkie on every Garda's hip in Galway city was fully charged. The whole station at Mill St. was quiet. There were lulls like this when nothing would happen and then there were other times when the whole switchboard would light up like the front of the fuckin' Seapoint. There had only been two calls in the last half hour. Kevin Sheehy from Rahoon had been in to say that someone was using his phone betting number with Paddy Power and was putting on bets for him. He was a bit steamed, but not annoyed. He just wanted to see what could he do about it. And after all, the horses had won.
Then some other fella from Henry Street came in to say that he had gotten a bad Chinese takeaway and that he wanted to prosecute the Chink for food poisoning. He even had the remains of the meal in a bag and he kept shoving it in Garda Fogarty's face.
'Arragh go on, Guard, arrest the fuck. Five pounds he took off me for this. Not a bit o' chicken in it. It's all stalks,' he said picking up a bamboo shoot and waving it through the front desk window. Fogarty was starving and this was the last thing he needed, so he told him to fuck off. And he did. And then Fogarty went back upstairs to the Communications Room and let the others off for their break.

He hated the Galway Arts Festival and the crowd it brought to town.
'Shower of fuckin' wasters' he called them. Brought nothing but trouble. Just when you were getting ready for the Races and all kinds of ordinary decent chancers, the town gets full of all sorts of strange fuckers doing all sorts of strange tricks on the streets and making it easy for the pickpockets.
It was one of them who stabbed him with a syringe the previous year and had him sweating for three months. It wasn't funny. He had lain

Nightmusic

awake at night for months thinking about what if he had Aids and what if he died because some fucker had stuck a syringe into him. He didn't go near Mary for the three months in case he had anything. Which he didn't. But nobody ever compensated him for the nights of terror, though. Just because he was a Garda, it seems 'twas OK that his mind should be messed up by it all. If he got the bollocks again, he'd fuckin' strangle him. German puppeteer picking pockets and handbags.
Street theatre they called it. Street theatre me hole, he thought. Dark alley, dark night, and the same fucker would be waking up with a crowd around him. A crowd of fuckin' surgeons. And picking up his teeth with broken fingers.
He looked at the clock on the station wall and peered out the window across at the houses on Nun's Island. It just dawned on him that he'd never seen a nun over there. He knew they were down there somewhere. A crowd of them who hadn't spoken for years and years, probably going around nodding at one another. There'd never been a call-out to a row there anyway, he thought. Hidden away behind glass they are, like panda bears, their dark and white shapes moving behind the frosted glass. He wondered should he bring down the dried bamboo shoots from the Chinese meal and pass it through the bars to them. He laughed at the thought of it and continued reading the *Advertiser*, even though the top of it was missing now and lost more pieces every time he turned a page. He went to the used car section. The one all Guards love, but the phone buzzed and he fitted on the ear-piece only to hear the line go dead. He hated calls like that. They could be a prank or it could be some poor aul wan struggling to get to the phone. Or it could just be a wrong number. You never knew. You just never knew, even though they had caller display.
He looked up at the clock again. It was still hot in here. And quiet.
2 a.m. Time for the grub. Time to get the squad car to hunt for grub. Time to use technology to catch fish and chips. Even though he shouldn't, because he was getting too fat, but fuck the calories. There's good fat and bad fat, and his was the good stuff.
Quigley, the Super, had warned them about making smart comments and swearing on the radios or belittling the force.
'There are people out there with scanners who can hear ye, so smarten it up,' he said to them at the station meeting at the start of May when he was telling them of his plans for a clean up summer in Galway. No fighting or brawling or killing. Straight run through to September when

Nightmusic

all the festivals would be over and, so above all, the force had to set standards and keep to them.
The Super would not agree with food being ordered over the radio.
The Super wanted them to use the landlines or their mobiles to communicate personal stuff like that, but that would take time and anyway, Fogarty needed to find a car heading back to Mill Street and past a Supermac's.
The Super would not have liked this, but then again, the Super was at home tucked up in bed, so fuck him.
'Golf Alpha,'
He waited for the reply.
'Go ahead, Noel.'
'Are ye passing Supermac's? Over.'
'Mebbe,' came the reply. 'Are ya askin'?'
'I'm asking.'
'We're passin'.
' Get me a fishbox. Over.'
'A fishbox. Who do you think we are? Captain Bird's Eye, is it? Over.'
'And a can of Coke. Over.'
'And a leg of fish, is it? Over.'
'Well if it is, I'll kick your hole with it. Over and out.'
The Super twisted in his sleep.

Fogarty took up the paper again and looked down through the used cars.
1989 Audi for £1,200. Black. One careful owner. Genuine reason for selling.
He grunted at that. Sure wasn't every car sold for a genuine reason? The fuckin' arse could be gone in it. Isn't that a genuine reason?

When the phone buzzed the next time, Fogarty didn't know what to make of it. It had been diverted through by the 999.
The woman sounded drunk and hysterical and was bawling into the phone.
'Calm down love, and tell me what happened.'

Marilyn Carstein had been staying in the new hotel by the bridge and had gone for a late stroll with her husband. She wanted to smell the Claddagh air and even though it was dark, she wanted to see where the

sun went down over Galway Bay. Ronnie, her husband, thought this was bullshit, but he didn't care. He wanted to fart a lot anyway, so the Claddagh air could take it better than room 410. She had wanted to feed the swans who she could barely make out below at the side.
Ronnie wasn't into swans.
Lazy overfed fuckin' seagulls, he called them, but then Ronnie used the adjectives 'lazy' and 'fuckin'' about a lot of categories, including the Irish.
They'd had a meal in the little French restaurant on Quay Street earlier and had asked for a bag of bread bits for the swans. But the swans weren't hungry. She threw them a scrap of the crusts, but only one of them was bothered to go after it. Marilyn was disappointed. She'd heard about Irish swans in a Frank McCourt book and how hungry they were supposed to be. But that was Limerick and this is Galway. By that rate, they should be the fastest growing swans in Europe, but they continued to ignore her gesture.
'Fuck them, babe,' said Ronnie. 'They'll be there in the morning?' But she ignored him and threw in another piece of bread.
Two of them were nudging their beaks at a sack of something. It was when she leant down to empty the bag of crumbs that she let the scream out of her, startling the swans and making them splash their way out into the middle of the river, wings full out and leaving behind what they'd been chewing on, the bloated corpse of a young woman, with her eyes looking upward and her mouth open and the skin on one side of her face flapping in and out like the lining on a torn jacket.

* * * *

Nightmusic

'Such an event is indicative of the moral decline of our society, would you say? You could see the strands of Bosnia in that. You could see where that all began in that piece. I thought it was fascinating, didn't you?'

Reporter Davy Morley nodded while the arts writer withered on. He hated the fuckin' Galway Arts Festival as well, especially because it brought all these wankers into town. Galway was great — when you had it to yourselves. It was your patch, where if anything happened it was your story and your right to send it off to the national papers. The city itself is a delight at 10 in the morning, but as the day moves on, you feel you're losing it, you're handing it over to the blow-ins and the visitors and then it's not so nice. And Arts Festival and Races time were like that because you had to grin at everyone and say, 'Jaysus isn't this a great town for partying? God we're really like this all the time ya know. Especially when the chance of any decent story you could send off to the nationals was reduced because they all had their own crowd down. And the arts writers were the worst, but you had to talk to them. You'd never know when you could be looking for a job in the *Irish Times*. He knew they didn't give a shite what the hack from the local paper thought. They'd just prefer if he nodded so they could get on with their bullshit but it gave them someone to philosophise to.

'Yes, Bosnia. Moral decline. Yes,' replied Morley.

'You see, too much of Irish art is concerned with our past, Christian Brothers, buggery, rampant republicanism and this sort of material delves deeper into what really causes conflict.' Morley wanted to yawn so badly, He wanted to yawn so that his mouth would envelop his whole head and so that he could sleep, but his mouth was full of red wine and a horrible dry vol au vent, so he couldn't. He also wanted Jim Anderson to fuck off. Life was too short to be spent talking to an arts critic from the *Times*. He wished too that he could spit out this dry vol au vent with its hummus filling and get over to Supermac's for some decent food. And he wished he was in bed.

But in an act of amazing telepathy, local poet and alcoholic Colman Kelly rescued the situation. Kelly had never appeared at the Arts Festival as an artist, yet he was always the one giving the creative writing classes in Galway, another fuckin' dreamer which the city is full of. He stepped over and told the arts critic from the *Times* that he was talking through his hole and that the show was 'a loadabolloxandawasteoftaxpayersmoney andcorporatecodswallop.'

Nightmusic

But Anderson wasn't too ruffled. He fixed his bowtie and hoped the little man would go away.

'Kelly, don't be venting your spleen on me. This wouldn't have anything to do with the fact you didn't get your Arts Council grant last year for that, ah so called collection. Would it?'

Morley stepped back to dodge the shower of spittle.

'Anderson, you're only a bullshitter and this was shite. Utter scutter.'

'Oh piss off, you annoying Philistine.'

At that Kelly grabbed the Dublin journo and pinned him up against the wall, sending wine and vol au vent all over Morley.

'Don't you call me a fuckin' Palestinian.'

The two men fell into a heap on the floor of the marquee, the poet having the upper hand as Anderson struggled to find a place for his now empty glass but then the man from the *Times* recovered his composure to knee the poet in the balls. Morley reckoned it was some sort of martial arts move that the *Times* man had learned while on coffee break from D'Olier Street. Some complicated yoga move. Or maybe 'twas just an old fashioned knee in the balls.

Anderson's knee.

Handy to have.

For the Times we live in.

Arts Festival officials rushed over. The press officer not knowing what to say, but getting his priorities right and opting to help the *Times* man up first anyway.

Morley wanted to go in and help Kelly up, but he couldn't be arsed and anyway, he had his tickets for the rest of the week to worry about. No point taking sides. Especially a losing side.

He decided to leave. He couldn't be caught in these situations again. It was only a few months since he was pictured at a rave night which was raided by the cops and the Chief at the *Chronicle* had hauled him over the coals about it.

'How can we be an upstanding local paper if our representatives are found in places like that? Now I'm not going to ask you if you were partaking, but I hope you fuckin' weren't. You'll be out on your ear.'

Morley loved having a Chief who had a reputation for being a bollocks. The whole country is littered with local papers that have guys who were supposed to be bastards at the helm. They aren't really, but it was still a great feeling to have your own bollocks. And one of the best.

Nightmusic

When he got out of the tent at Fisheries Field and found his car in the Cathedral carpark, he scratched his receding hairline, glad to be out of the conversation with Anderson. He leaned over and pushed the CD button. 'I'm your forever friend,' roared out Charlie Landsborough. Fuck. He thought he'd taken that one out. The music pages were due in next morning, he was supposed to have reviewed that album. Good job he didn't have a bird in the car tonight with that bursting into action. He'd look like a right prick. Arts and music critic for the local paper playing Charlie Landsborough. Imagine the headline — 'Local arts writer likes Liverpool crap.' Arts and music critic as well as being news writer and sports writer and feature writer and a bit of everything really. There was no place for titles like Anderson's in local newspapers. There were more CDs under the seat, but 'twas too much bother to get them. Then he thought of the scanner in the dash. He'd bought it from a company in Wexford a few years earlier. They got a consignment of them in from Holland and they were great. Of course, they weren't as much use now as they were in the days of the 088 analogue phones. Then it was around the clock conversations, like the one where he heard the knacker telling his wife to grunt for him to add authenticity to his wank. And there were others like the old pair having the affair in Glenamaddy who he'd listen to every night. But now, 'twas only the Guards and the Fire Brigade and the odd airplane into Carnmore. He leaned over and pulled it out, setting the frequency to between 164 and 165 and letting it search. He knew the guards in the city had a different frequency to the ones in the country, but if anything happened, he'd pick it up here. As he drove back across the Salmon Weir bridge, headed for Supermac's, he laughed as Fogarty told the cops in the car he'd kick their arses with the leg of fish and turned the car towards the N17 and home. But he was only two miles out when he heard the call to the cars to forget the fishbox and get to the Claddagh. He'd never done a hand brake turn before, but now he did. And it seemed so easy.

* * * *

The Super got the call about 4 a.m. He debated whether or not to come in. He called Fogarty back.
'The Fire Brigade got her out, Super. And Malachy Lee helped as well with his boat. She'd been there for a while. The eels had done their bit and I'd say...'

Nightmusic

'Yes, Fogarty, that's enough. I'll see the report in the morning. No-one on the lost list, is there?'
'I don't think so, sir.'
'I'll be in at 8 and we'll take it from there. Is the body gone to the hospital?'
'Yes sir,'
'Declared dead, I presume?'
Fogarty wanted to reply 'as dead as a fuckin' dodo' but he thought better of it and just said, 'Affirmative.' Great word that.
It means yes and you could use it for lots of things. Pity there was nothing affirmative about his fish and chips

It was 4 a.m. and Fogarty was still fuckin' starving, but for some reason or other, he was gone off the idea of the fish box. A chicken box would have to do. Not so much of the nautical about it.
But even that was off the menu as Supermac's was closed. So it was a soft Marietta biscuit from the canteen and a cup of tea that would have to keep him going until he clocked off at 6.

A jumper is no good of a story. Morley realised that as soon as he got to the Claddagh. The Guards nodded at him. They'd seen him covering court before, and gave him the Garda look — the look that says 'We know where you fuckin' live.' That's the thing about the Guards, They want to know everything. They want to know what you drive, how old she is, how much ya got her for, who you work for, how much you're earning, who you're shaggin' and whether you have any previous. It bugs them to hell altogether when you have no previous or you have nothing unusual about ya at all. There's nothing so annoying for a Guard than to know nothing about ya.
'Another student. Nothing in that. Nawthing in that for you or even for me.'
Morley knew there was nothing in it for the *Chronicle*. They didn't touch suicides, because some advertiser or other would be related and there was some unwritten code about suicides. For years the words 'foul play is not suspected' had said it all, A fella could have shot himself and hanged himself and stabbed himself through the heart and still all you could say was 'foul play is not suspected.' Great line that, but people were getting wise to that now and were reading between the lines, reading too much perhaps, so it was better to give them the full

gore.

But if the *Chronicle* weren't going to touch it, the tabloids would pay him £30 a shot for it in the morning, especially if it was written up in a 'Body of a young woman was taken from the river Corrib' style. The words body and young woman in any sentence were enough to get any editorial loins stirring, so he took out the laptop and waited for it to boot up in the back of the car and typed with one hand and ate chips with the other.

* * * *

Nightmusic

Up in Mayo, Frank and Catherine Sheridan got up round 7.30 and he let out the dog.

He'd been barking since around 4 o'clock on and off. They reckoned it must have been that cat from across the road again. Cheeky little bugger. He'd run across the garden and then walk back past the patio door where the dog was sleeping.

He now knew the dog could not get through the glass. Frank thought about how the cat would have come to ascertain this and that it must have taken some nerve for him to find it out in the first place. Of course, the dog went ape-shit peering through the glass at the cat who just sat there on the other side of the pane and licked his paws, his back and all the way back to his hole, which I suppose after all was the cat's way of saying, 'Up yours, Fido.' But now the dog was out and there was no sign of the cat. Frank didn't mind getting up early anyway as he was going fishing that day on Lough Mask with the Germans. Twenty-five quid a day they were paying him to be their gillie. Bring them out around the best parts of the lake, tell them tall tales and feed them shite and they love ya for it. Especially if you brought them to the deep parts where they would depart with traditional Irish lake fishing methods and take out their echo sounder with which they could detect big fish.

Pike they were after.

Big fuckers with heads the size of dogs.

The pikes that is, not the Germans.

They'd sit for hours watching their echo sounder and then when the big bleep would come on it, they'd lower the big baits and wait for the mother of all battles. The first time Frank saw the gear he thought they were going to use depth charges to blow the fish out of the water and he thought this was great crack. Far better than gillying for Northern Irish or Scots who wouldn't give ya a fright. But the Germans were great and every Christmas there'd be a big box of chocolates and clothes from Berlin.

The same Germans had been coming to them for over 20 years and now they were bringing new ones who would then come at other times of the year, so his season was spreading and there'd be more money and more chocolate, more clothes and more fun. He knew he wasn't charging them all the full £25. He knew some of them didn't have a pot to piss in, but they were generous when they came, bringing the odd outboard engine or fishing tackle for him, so he'd return the favour.

Nightmusic

They wanted to go fishing at 6 a.m., but Frank wouldn't have it. He said call at nine and we'll see. So the Germans would go off without him and then come back in for him later. He scratched at his head, looked in the fridge, but there wasn't anything there for a decent sandwich, so he decided to go down to the shop and get a few slices of ham and a head of lettuce. He went into the back hall and pulled on his waders, but had forgotten to shake them out beforehand and so had to take them off and take the stones out of them. He had one on when he heard the doorbell ring. 'Jaysus, it couldn't be the Germans yet.' He told them nine o'clock. Do they not understand English? Maybe not. You were never too early for them and if you said you weren't ready they'd almost come in and watch you atin' your breakfast.
He had the second wader on when he heard the commotion at the kitchen door and heard his wife gasp, and give a little moan.
He stood up in the boots when Sgt. Tierney came in. The Germans, it must be the Germans. Had something happened to them? He didn't want them going out on the lake on their own. They said they wouldn't go out far and now they must have and hit a rock and broke the shaft on the outboard and got drowned or something.
'Martin, what is it?'
'Frank, Catherine. I have some bad news for ye. It's about Nicola. In Galway.'

The Germans were very understanding when they called to the house for Frank. They stayed a while, asked if there was anything they could do before leaving, taking Frank up on the offer of the boat for the day, but they too were a bit too upset to think about fishing. Dieter, the oldest of them, had a son who was killed in a crash driving in Poland in 1985 so he knew a little about what it was like, but he didn't have enough English to offer any consolation to Frank. He passed it on through his eyes.
Frank felt cold in the kitchen. He'd have loved to have gone on the lake with them now. Yesterday, the thought of spending a day trying to make conversation with them was daunting and was getting him down. But now he wished he could only have yesterday's worries back again. And Nicola.
He thought back to when he saw her last. 'I'll see ya next week, Dad,' she had said as she left the house on Sunday night. He had offered to take her to the bus, but she wanted to walk herself, carrying her

rucksack full of fresh clothes. She had told Catherine she wanted new running gear and when he offered her the money, she said she'd wait until her birthday arrived two weeks later. He thought to himself that he'd a have a few more quid then from the Germans and he'd be able to buy her something else nice as well. He loved treating her. She'd been long enough arriving after they married but she'd made every day since then worthwhile. She went out to work in Molloy's Supermarket when she was only 14 and had never really asked them for much money. She knew deep down that her Dad wanted a son and she made him forget that by learning about football and hurling and soccer and she made a point of watching the World Cup and the Olympics with him. It only seemed like yesterday when he drove her to Ballinrobe to get the newspaper to see if she had gotten her place in college. The first one in their family. Ever. She had told him her CAO number and she watched with intrigue as his rough eyes scanned the pages for the number which told him she was going to Galway.

Catherine stirred back in the room. He knew she wasn't sleeping, just lying on the bed sobbing, the tablets the doctor prescribed doing the trick. He had gone in and put his arm on her shoulder, but he felt there would be people coming, calling, shaking hands, asking questions, shaking heads and the place had to be tidied up. And he was still in his socks.
He could remember the door closing the previous Sunday as their only child headed away. The glass in the panels shaking as she made her way out, pulling it firmly, the way she used to. She had smiled. Yes, he remembered that. She smiled as she went out. And now she was dead. How could she be? She didn't have any worries, but something must have led her to do what she did. Was she pregnant? He'd like to ask Catherine if she knew anything. Catherine dealt with her regarding all those things. The sanitary towels were always placed discreetly on the top shelf in the hot press, where Frank was not supposed to see them and where Catherine would put two new packs every month. He'd ask Catherine if she knew anything like that, but she was lying down now for a while. It was late afternoon and soon her sisters would be here and Frank's brothers and the house would never be the same again. What was normally calm would become hectic and then get incredibly quiet. Sgt. Tierney had been sound when he came in. He didn't push them on anything, but just asked them if she had any problems. Or if she had

any boyfriend. Or if she was on any form of medication. But Frank didn't know. And neither did Catherine. They knew she had seen a doctor in the college about some headaches she was having and that she had difficulty sleeping, but beyond that, they didn't know. All they knew is that now, they were alone in the world again, just as they had been before Nicola became the light of their life. And now she was dead.

Drowned in a Galway river.

With her face eaten away.

Maybe by a fish with a head on him like a dog.

* * * *

Nightmusic

Judge Keane wanted to know who had farted out loud during his summing up.

Everyone knew where it had come from but nobody could do anything. The judge looked up at the gallery full of gurriers but did not know whether to make a comment or let it go. The young Garda standing up made some move to find the culprit, but a dirty look from the Super told him to get back and not to be making a fool of himself.

The Judge looked down at Morley and the others in the press bench, right under his own seat.

'That one was certainly released without bail, would you say?' he said to the clerk. Now everyone could laugh, and they did and then he continued with his summing up.

Morley hated covering courts on Fridays.

Especially the never-ending cases about knackers fighting in the streets stripped to the waist and all sharing the same name. These went on for ever as brother after sister after aunt after uncle had to go on the stand and give a different version of what had happened.

And now the place was full of them. One entire side of the District Courthouse was filled with them, all with fuck all else to do but learn the law. You'd pass out afterwards and hear the Guards talking about football and the solicitors talking about golf and the biggest crowd of all would be the knackers talking about recognizances being fixed in the event of an appeal and of how a certain course of legal action might sway a case.

The court ended just in time to allow him to get to the office to get his cheque. Twenty to five in the evening, giving him barely enough time to get to the bank and cash it. Morley loved his job. He'd always wanted to be a journalist but now he was one he couldn't believe how easy it was. The *Chronicle* came out every Wednesday so they got a half day there; Thursday was spent doing music reviews and the children's column; Friday was the day for features or interviews. Monday was a doss day to chat with the others about the matches at the weekend, then hop to Galway to cover a County Council or Health Board meeting. Tuesday was supposed to be the busiest day of the week when the paper went to bed but it never reached cardiac arrest and then it was Wednesday again. He realised his whole life was disappearing in a host of Tuesdays. But he loved Tuesdays. He wished it could be Tuesday every day. It was the one day that he was being set

Nightmusic

a challenge to go out and get four or five stories, come back, write them up and present them to the newsdesk at teatime. If you were lucky, they were accepted without much change and you could go home. But if you were really lucky you got to stay behind when the real business of putting a paper together swung into action. He loved being there when the template for the front page was opened up on screen and when the drawing of the fake front page would be scribbled onto a sheet of blank paper. He loved seeing his stories being taken in and more often than not being given the headline he had chosen for them. And he loved seeing his name in bold type underneath each one.

But even Tuesdays had to end and when he'd troop home at nine o'clock leaving the production team to put the finishing touches to the paper, he felt that he still was not spent, that there was more he could do, that it was hard to believe there would not be another deadline again until this time next week.
And that's why he did 'corr.'
That and the sterling cheques which fell onto the mat of his flat every month.

Corr, short for correspondence, is the name given by aged hacks to stories written for the national papers by reporters from the regions. There was a great tradition of corr in the *Chronicle*. The west was always a great picking ground for three-legged asses or singing dog stories. Anything wild could happen out west and the nationals just lapped it up.
While the stories may not be as quirky nowadays, there is still a great demand for stories west of the Shannon. Some of the midlands reporters had told him once that he was lucky to work in the west, as nothing quirky ever happened in the midlands.
'The damp ground seems to seep all the creativity and energy out of the fuckers, not like the West, where you could find a German rocket scientist in the darkest corner of Connemara or a member of some top rock band living on an island in Mayo,' he said.
Morley liked this town now too, even though at different times, it loved him and then hated him and then loved him again.
It was only 20 minutes from Galway so, effectively, he dipped into whatever stories the city spewed up as well. And while the country areas had the monopoly on the rare three-legged donkey stories, the

city invariably provided the more regular supply of juicier tales.

He picked up the tabloids. They were still running with a few short pieces on the body of the young girl washed up in the Claddagh. He spread them on the table in the kitchen and counted them. £30 for that one. £40 for that and £25 for another. But £25 in sterling. The guts of a ton made for one day's work and one small story. Who'd be bothered writing long complicated features when you could make as much from briefs? He took a sip from his pint. The pub was quiet for a Friday evening and he counted the stories again and thought about how every one of those figures represented a major misery in someone's life and yet they represented some sort of triumph for him, the triumph of getting the story in before some other hack.

But like those dreams you have of doom and gloom when you're a kid, he just brushed the dark thoughts out of his mind and went to the sports pages to see if Arsene Wenger had bought anyone for Arsenal.

* * * *

Nightmusic

Malachy Lee was born in the family home at 3, St. Joseph's Terrace, Shantalla on January 27th, 1956, the 200th anniversary of the birth date of Wolfgang Amadeus Mozart. However, wee Malachy didn't know it at the time. Nobody in the room shared that with him. They had other things on their mind. It was a full nine years before he realised who he shared his birthdate with and then only because he saw it in the famous birthdays section in the *Irish Press*.

A heavy frost fell that morning and Dr. Gannon who came to the house to deliver him, fell twice on the way, but Malachy's father said that he'd come straight from the barstool, so 'twas no wonder he nearly broke his hole on the path outside. Delia Lee's screams could be heard down the street but Nora Kennedy held her hand throughout and directed the other neighbours in their busy assembly line of hot water, towels and holy medals. Delia who had come originally from out past Furbo, had already lost one child, a daughter, after the umbilical cord became wrapped around the infant's neck. And given the trouble she'd had with this pregnancy, the neighbours and Dr. Gannon weren't expecting much better. But despite their pessimism and Dr. Gannon's sore arse, just after 2 in the morning, the bloodied body of little Malachy slithered from between the legs of Delia into the arms of the doctor and inhaled the first whiffs of beer from his stubbled chin.

The first and only child of Delia and Paddy, Malachy was soon besotted with the life of Mozart. Like the composer, he followed his father into the business, but while Leopold Mozart was a talented musician who brought his son on tours of the courts of Europe, Paddy Lee worked on the fishing boats, helped out on the ships coming into the docks, fished for mackerel at dusk and brought his son on a tour of the dockside pubs where Malachy would sit and sip diluted orange drinks while Paddy and the others sank pints and talked grown-up shite.

But the shite-talking ended suddenly one March evening in 1968. Malachy was twelve and Paddy was extolling the virtues of the Galway three-in-a- row team when he gave a great yelp out of him, then a moan and fell back off the stool onto the floor. The others who were there with him said that the heart attack killed him before he hit the floor and cracked his head open, but how the fuck did they know? Malachy was in the back room throwing a solitary dart at a tattered dart board, supping at the bottom of his long-drained glass when they came through to get him and bring him home. He didn't know why they did that or why there was a sheet over something on the floor of the bar or why his mother started screaming when they got there. They just took him by the hand and led him down Shantalla to the house and then pushed him aside into one room with a tuppenny bit in his hand. He remembered the funeral though — the men in the black coats coming to the house to tip their hats at the coffin where his father lay with a great purple head on him and a white bandage around his forehead, still and silent inside a coffin, left appropriately enough, on four large Guinness crates in the front room.

After that everything changed in the house. Of course, they got to bed a lot earlier because Paddy wasn't coming home roaring like an eejit, and calling the McGintys next door a shower of Mayo cunts, but the house was a lot quieter. The people who used to come calling to pick him up or drop him home or see if he could pay them they money he owed them, stopped calling around. Even the owner of the pub where he died wrote a note saying he was going to wipe his slate clean, but Delia wrote back and told him to shove it up his arse, except not in those words of course, because she was a lady.

It was around this time that Malachy started as an altar boy even though he had to wear a soutane and surplice used by some of the boys from St. Mary's College. It was Father Curtin who got them for him and who got him his place in the C group. The garments were a bit too big for him, but Delia stitched them up with the help of Nora Kennedy and made them look just right. Father Curtin used to call to the house to comfort Delia but most of the time, he just bothered her as she'd have to get the best china down and always keep a packet of Kerry Creams in the press in case he'd call, which he did with alarming regularity. Malachy loved helping out in the sacristy with the musty smell of the altar wine and the talcumy smell of the priests. It was here that Father Curtin told him that the only way to get on in life was by reading books and he presented Malachy with a card allowing him to join the town library for free. 'Sherlock Holmes, Malachy, the best detective in the world. There are stories in there that will make your hair curl even more. You'll never look at a dog the same way again after reading *The Hound of The Baskervilles*,' he said to Malachy. And so down Malachy went to the library and clambered up on the elevated section where the children's books were and sat there for days on end, reading about

Nightmusic

great adventures by men seeking to reach the South Pole, about Hillary and Tensing on the mountain, about the discovery by Howard Carter of the Tutankhamen treasures in Egypt. He went through about twenty of the Sherlock Holmes books early on too, but perhaps most of all, he read about the man he shared his birth date with — Wolfgang Amadeus Mozart.

He thought Wolfgang was a classy name, much classier than Malachy Lee. There were lots of other Lees in Galway and even in Shantalla but there were damn all Mozarts. He asked Father Curtin if he could take the name Wolfgang for his confirmation but the priest said no and told him not to be having such daft ideas. There was no Saint Wolfgang and anyway that's more a name for a dog than a person, he said. Mother wouldn't go for it either, but Malachy had the last laugh as on the day Bishop Browne tapped him on the shoulder up in the Cathedral, Malachy said the name Wolfgang in his mind instead of the Colm his mother had given him and so unknown to himself, the Bishop had just confirmed a Wolfgang in the eyes of God. The first Wolfgang in Galway.

However, despite reading everything there was to know about Mozart, it was not until he was fourteen that he actually heard his first piece of Mozart, the Piano Sonata No. 11 in A K333 — the *Rondo Alla Turca (Allegretto)*. It was playing on a record player in the living quarters of the *Grecco Luccinni*, an Italian ship docked below in the harbour with a load of coal. When he heard it first he thought it was someone in there playing a piano, it sounded so real, but then it hopped and skipped. Still, its quirky hopping movement and jauntiness made him yearn to play an instrument like that. It was only when he picked up the needle and watched the record and its red label slow down that he saw it was by Mozart. So he wound the handle again and let it play away, the skip and all. But it wasn't long before he was caught in there and was run out of it by a fat Italian with a day's growth of beard and a bottle of whiskey who told him what was probably the equivalent of 'fuck off' in Italian.

Up in Father Curtin's house one day he took a quick look through his record collection to see if he had any Mozart. But he hadn't. He had lots of Delia Murphy stuff, *The Spinning Wheel* and *Three Lovely Lassies from Bannion*, Doc Carroll singing *Ol' Man Trouble*, Jimmy O'Dea singing *Red Sails In The Sunset*, some Bridie Gallagher stuff, but

Nightmusic

no foreign music, nothing to match the beauty of Mozart. Maybe Fr Curtin only had stuff from people whose names were saints. He looked in Ingrams' shop down town, but he could never get close enough to the record sleeves as it was normally crowded with students from the university who talked to each other about the music, and anyway, anytime the shop assistant saw him looking through the records, she'd come over and ask him if there was anything in particular he was looking for, and he knew he couldn't answer and just say Mozart, because he couldn't afford to buy it and he didn't have a record player, and he'd get embarrassed and leave, which is what she wanted to achieve anyway. It was hard enough to sell classical records without scruff like that looking though them and probably bending the sleeves. He saw Mozart's name on a poster in Newcastle one day, advertising a concert being held up in the college by the music society and he bought a ticket in Powells and went along. He'd never been inside the university before, and its ivy-covered arches intimidated him as if he was entering some sort of forbidden place. The concert was held in a high ceiling-ed room with a soft yellow light. He was eighteen at this stage and was earning his own money on the ships and with the mackerel. Almost everyone there that night was about his own age, or maybe a bit older and they all had a copy of the programme. So he went out and got one and read about each of the pieces that were being played by the visiting orchestra.

It was on this night that he first heard the *Overture* from *The Marriage of Figaro* and he was transfixed by it, much more so than the others who were there, he thought. He nearly jumped out of his seat at the first blast of sound in it but knew when it was coming around again and soon he found the tune winging its way around in his head. So this is what appreciating music is all about, he thought, learning the music and knowing which way it's going to go. He was excited by this and by the three nice girls from the college who came in late, each carrying a pile of books and sat near to him. But when he got home, Mother didn't want to hear about the concert. All she wanted to know was how he'd gotten on at the docks and whether he'd be going out for mackerel instead of going to the library and reading all the time. She was always on at him to go out and visit his uncle Peadar in Furbo 'so that he might leave ya a bit of land and so you can make something of yourself,' but he preferred to go to the library. One night, she'd taken his library books

Nightmusic

and burnt them so that he wouldn't be able to go back down there again without getting a fine. He heard her creeping into the room, taking the books and then a minute later, the clatter of the range door as it was slammed shut on the furnace and the reddening pages inside. He said he'd never forget that. She never had time for books anyway. But he told them in the library that the dog had chewed the books really badly and that he'd pay for them and so he did, just a little bit every week and within a few weeks, he was back in there again reading and bringing home books and hiding them in a bag under the floorboards.

Mother would have killed him if she knew he attended the Protestant bazaar down Ardilaun Road. It was a bright sunny day and the people were drinking homemade lemonade and playing all sorts of strange games that only Protestants can understand. But he didn't want any games. He wanted to spend all the time at the book stall run by the little old lady with the old but pretty face. He spent nearly a pound on secondhand books, mostly other Sherlock Holmes ones the librarian couldn't be bothered to get for him, like the early ones. He didn't want these to get thrown in the range, so he brought them up the attic, only bringing one down at a time whenever he wanted to read it again and again. He knew she'd never be up there, so they were safe from her claws, in the bag right above her bedroom. Then at night, he'd read through them under the sheets with a small torch he had and imagine he was Holmes.

That Holmes spoke lovely, so he did, and Watson, even though he was a doctor, was always amazed by Holmes' sayings, so they must have been good. He imagined he was being chased by the hound, that he was pursuing Moriarty, that he and Watson were after discovering a body and that Mother was Mrs. Hudson, their landlady at 221B Baker Street. In morningtime, when he'd be getting up for the same feed of overdrawn tea and brown bread, he'd push himself out of the bed, wash his face and say to himself in the mirror, *'Watson, Mrs. Hudson has risen to the occasion. Her cuisine is a little limited, but she has as good an idea of breakfast as a Scotchwoman,'* whatever that meant, but it sounded good.

When the library moved to Augustine Street, his life became a lot easier because he could go in there and read any day it was slack on the docks. And there were lots of those days. It was only a short walk from the docks to the Hynes Building and you'd always find him down at one of the cubicles in the far corner of the library, in between biography and the sciences with a packet of Emerald sweets, in the green packet. Of course, Mother doesn't bother him anymore about bringing home books, but she shouldn't have done that to him when he was younger. The auld bitch shouldn't have done it, he told himself over and over again. A lesser man might become affected by it.

* * * *

Nightmusic

It took Morley nearly an hour to get back from Mayo.
Mainly because he stopped on the way to hook his laptop onto his mobile and e-mail the copy to Dublin, Cork and Belfast. It had been a sad funeral. Sadder than any of the other ones he'd covered in the past. The Sheridans were devastated. Normally he didn't get emotional at these, but this one was very bad as Nicola was an only child. He'd snuck in and sat at the back of the choir where he fitted in among the latecomers and recorded the sermon on the dictaphone. Tragic funerals were a doddle to cover. All you wanted were a few paras from the sermon, the names of the priests, the gifts that were brought up and any particular type of music that was being played, especially in murder funerals, but this was different. Normally, in suicides, the papers wouldn't touch them, but this was still a death under investigation so they wanted ten or twelve paras, ya know the usual 'The community was united in grief' shit' ... and so on.
He rang each newsroom to confirm that the e-mail had been received. It had, but they said that they weren't sure how much they could use, given the nature of the death. But he'd get paid for it anyway, so he shut the laptop and had a Chinese for his lunch in Claremorris. Chicken szechuan with fried rice and a Diet Coke and he took his time with it.

Back in the newsroom there was great hilarity when he walked through the door.
Terry Fahy was studying the form and giving his tips.
The photos of the Queen of Galway were in the *Chronicle* this week and as usual, Fahy had been out with four or five of them.
'See yer wan there?'
'Who?'
'Rosaleen Shiel.'
Yeah, what about her?'
'She's up the spout.'
'You're joking and she's in this?'
'Yeah.'
'What'll happen if she wins it?'
'Dunno.'
'Who did the dirty deed?'
'Mark Darcy, ponsy fucker.'
'So he did it, did he?'
'Yeah. It seems he overshot the runway.'

Fahy had been in the *Chronicle* for three years more than Morley. He had come from a journalism college however and was Student of the Year. That meant he had great shorthand, could type like a train, knew his Irish cúpla focal, had a good phone manner, but couldn't write for shite. He wouldn't know a good story if it jumped up and bit him on the bollocks. Still, he was great crack and had been up on half the women in the town.

'Look,' he'd say on a Monday morning, lifting up his shirt and exposing his back.

'See that scrape?'

'Yeah.'

'That's Moira Moloney.'

'And have ye ever seen clawmarks on an arse?'

'No, and we don't want to either,' said Tim Logan, the elder lemon in the newsroom.

Tim was the one who had seen John F. Kennedy in Galway. He wasn't a journalist then but he wanted to be one. He was the *Chronicle*'s man about the place. The one who everyone knew, the man who went to every function in the area at a weekend and took down the name of everyone he saw there for printing in his column. His column was the greatest load of shite in Irish journalism but more people read it than for the rest of the paper put together. It was 'Mary Kate was seen at the GAA do with Paddy Joe' and so on. It was a libel minefield but it was popular and it was one way of ensuring buffs kept reading the paper and didn't just look at the pictures.

Aoife Collins was not in the newsroom for Fahy's exhibition, but it wouldn't have stopped him. She was the only woman on the news staff and was a great writer. She came in, took the fags out of her bag and lit up.

'So you're back.'

'I can see why you're a reporter. Powers of observation, is it?"

'Made a killing I suppose. The English cheques will be bouncing in from the redtops.'

'Ya shouldn't be doing freelance down there in Mayo. It's not your area,' said Logan.

'Arragh, fuck them.'

'In my day, you couldn't leave the town to do a story. Everyone had their area and that's the way it should be.'

'Tim, we're in the EU now. Freedom of Movement and all that. Have ya

Nightmusic

heard about the Bosman ruling?'
'Who. The Serbs is it?
'Ah, never mind. Let them come after me if they want. I was asked to do it and that's that.'

Morley's desk was just inside the door of the newsroom so he could hear everyone coming up the creaky stairs. Most people just ploughed on up, clattering each step with their heavy boots, but the Chief didn't. The Chief would have the door opened before you knew there was anyone there at all, the only concession to silence being his soft cough and shuffle before he opened the door. The Chief was in his 70s now and was not quite as fearsome as people outside would have you believe. Morley had been told that by others who had left the *Chronicle* that the Chief was an awesome bollocks, capable of stripping a giraffe with a tongue lashing. Some hacks had left because they couldn't stand the tension of not knowing when the next bollocking was coming along. But now he was getting old and slow and not quite capable of the fearsome outbursts he was renowned for. He only ever came into the newsroom however to make a proclamation. There was always some word of wisdom or some biting comment. He never came in for no reason at all. There was a purpose to his every journey around this rundown old building, just as there was today.
The door had opened and he was in before anyone had seen him.
'Listen up.'
All typing stopped.
'See this.'
He held up a sheet of paper with lots of handwriting on it. Handwriting is bad. Regular standard letters aren't handwritten. Only complaints are handwritten. Was it to be another letter of complaint like the time Morley had mistyped that a man had taken his dog 'for a wank on the prom' instead of 'a walk.' The Chief never bought that explanation. Fahy had changed it on Morley's screen just before it was laid onto the page and if the Chief knew, he'd have fired him, but Morley never squealed on him and Fahy was eternally grateful.
'This is a letter. A letter from a member of the public. What did I say about the public, eh Morley?'
'Yes, Chief, we must never underestimate the stupidity of the general public.'

Nightmusic

'That's right, Morley. Never let your guard down because just when you think that the general public can't stoop any lower, they come out and surprise you by going down even more.'

'Right, Chief.'

Now you know I always say that only fuckin' headers and cranks write to papers and that. Well, still remember that. That's why this is so important. It is a letter of thanks. It is from some fella who wanted me to put in a notice for his ceili and he wrote to say thanks. This is a thank you note,' he twirled around in his grey suit as if he were Perry Mason in a courtroom instead of a newsroom with just five reporters.

'And because it's a thank you note, I'm going to get it fuckin' framed. So today's lesson is if you get a thank you note, frame it.'

And with that he was out the door and back to his poky little office at the back of the building. An office piled high with old papers, journals and books and right in the middle of that there was the typewriter he refused to let go. The one on which he typed his editorials and then passed on to be re-set on computer. Morley breathed a sigh of relief when the Chief left. If he knew that he was gone all morning doing work for the national papers, he'd have had a fit, but the others had covered for him. At the dentist, he was supposed to have been. But for a split second Morley wondered if the Chief had rang the dentist and checked out his excuse. That split second had passed and the Chief was now out the door.

Because of his age, it was unlikely he'd make a second journey to this side of the building again today. He'd be there in the morning to open the mail in the boardroom and he'd take the opportunity to see them all and size them up and wonder if he had made a mistake in taking any of them on. He liked Morley. He was an unorthodox journalist like himself. None of this journalism training college or Diplomas. Morley had a nose for a story and even if he couldn't spell his name in shorthand, he was always hungry for a story and an angle. Morley had never asked how he got the name the Chief. It just seemed that all the others there over the years had called him that and now he liked it. If you met him in the corridor, you'd greet him with it. But despite all that, Morley didn't want to be caught sending stuff off to the national papers. The older lads in the newsroom had told him that in the 1970s, you had to tell the Chief what you were doing and he'd get the cheque and give you some of it. Which I suppose was only right given that he was paying the phone bill and that you wouldn't have gotten the story if you hadn't been on his staff. But today with e-mail and mobile phones, what he didn't know wouldn't bother him.

* * * *

Nightmusic

It was hot outside. It was always hotter in the city centre.
Malachy slid into the seat at the back of the Augustinian Church on Middle Street, knelt down and looked up at the wonderful colours. He loved it in here. It was always cool, even on the hottest day of the year, and with the sweat pouring off your head and into your eyes, you could come in here, sit down for a while and within minutes you'd be nicely cooled. He left his library books in a pile on the floor beside him and sat back in the seat. He'd read about churches being used as places of refuge in the Middle Ages and so it was here in Galway. And right in the heart of the city too. There were damp patches under the arms of his green tee-shirt, and what with his reddish hair and white arms, he looked like a tricolour.
Outside tourists were making their way out of Kennys' bookshop and gallery and across to Charlie Byrne's Bookshop. Educated-looking types, the ones who stopped to look at the art in Kennys' and who stroked their chins trying to let on they knew what the fuck the painting was about. Those types — the types who ate in all the strange foreign restaurants in the street, pushing strange looking food around their plates with knives, white wobbly stuff that looked like worms and flat dry pancake yolks that they tried to make some sort of a sandwich out of. You could tell them a mile off. They looked dirty but weren't. The men had ponytails and long beards and tweedy jackets like he had at home. And the women were auld ones, with wrinkled tanned faces and greying hair. Just like Protestant wimmen they were. You know the type you'd see organising fetes and bazaars and the likes. He recalled that Holmes had said to Watson in one of the books, *'art in the blood is liable to take the strangest forms,'* and so it must have with these people. They must have great jobs, he thought, to be able to go into Kennys' and restaurants and then sit outside and eat. Maybe they were on holidays, but he was sure he'd seen some of them around before. He slid over along the seat, far enough over to be right against the cool pillar. He laid a hand on it, pressed his wrist against it. He'd have loved to push his face against it, it was so cold, but he couldn't do that because there were others around.
Yes, he loved this church. He could imagine Mozart's *Mass in C Minor* rebounding off the walls in here, every high note climbing up the pillars and crawling around the ceiling, shattering and then falling down into the open ears below. He could imagine the soprano at the altar, her voice shooting out like a flame and getting into every corner. Mother

Nightmusic

had always gone to this church when she went to town. She'd come in for what seemed like an age and then go around to all the stations of the Cross and stop at each one and say a long prayer. He never liked that, walking around the church when there were people sitting in the seats. They were bound to be looking at ya and you looked liked a fuckin' eejit there with your mammy staring at the wall and her lips moving and nothing coming out. She did cruel things like that. Things that maybe she didn't know were cruel, but which were cruel nonetheless. Still, it's a lovely church. Very cool. He wiped another round of sweat from his forehead with the sleeve of his jumper and watched as the drops made a splatter on the front of his trousers.

They used to come to Mass here after Father died when she couldn't bring herself to go down to the Cathedral. The sermons were great here, a bit different from the normal run of the mill sermons they got from the Bishop in the Cathedral. Here they were more relevant and more craic. There was always a joke and a moral. He loved sermons with morals. They were the punchlines and they were supposed to make ya think, but they made him laugh. Inside, not out loud, of course.

He wondered what God would think about having a sinner in his house, but fuck it, weren't they all sinners, the auld ones queuing for confession and lighting candles, reaching for the top level in the vain hope that it might be that bit closer to heaven. But theirs were just pissy sins, not the real thing at all. They just had bad thoughts at bingo. Or cursed the cat. Nothing like he'd done.

He'd love to come in here some day and tell them all everything and see the reaction on their faces. Maybe the tourists would stop stroking their chins in Kennys' and come over and look at him and say in their strange accents 'Isn't he a great fuckin' man now for doing that and having the guts to tell us all.'

He knew they'd say that, so they would, and they'd be very impressed and they'd stop and stroke their chins even more and walk around him and marvel at him and wonder how they had gone for so long without knowing the genius that was in their midst.

Some day, he'd do that and that would be some day, it would. He'd explain how he did it all and never got caught. But then it wasn't something that Holmes would do. As he had said to Watson *'You know that a conjurer gets no credit when once he has explained his trick, and if I show you too much of my method of working, you will come to the conclusion that I am a very ordinary individual after all.'*

He reached over from his seat and took a handful of melted wax from the bottom of the candle holder. He lifted it to his nose and smelt it. He loved the smell of wax and the memories of mass serving it brought back. Other smells too. Smells of talcum powder and well pressed vestments; smells of cheap altar wine and incense used for the Benediction and sweat and other smells of Father Curtin. He loved serving up in St. Michael's, especially at the early morning masses when he'd run home afterwards and have slabs of brown bread freshly toasted on the fire by Mother who sat him in at the table and gave him his breakfast, the Man of the House, up early to bring home the bread, even though there was no pay for mass serving, it was his first real job and his borrowed soutane would be freshly pressed and washed but always smelt of camphor balls.

He was cool now. The sweat had stopped trickling out of some hole right in the middle of his head. It was time to get out into the sunshine again.

These hot days were great for tits.
There were lots of them out there.
Wobbling their way around the city
Waiting to be watched.

* * * *

Nightmusic

Superintendent Quigley walked back and forth across his office. He hated confrontation like this, but where disciplinary measures had to be taken, they had to be taken. He rang out for the secretary to ring down to the canteen and ask Garda Fogarty to come up. Again.

Noel Fogarty took the lift to the first floor of Mill St. station. He always felt like a prick taking a lift for one floor. He reckoned that maybe that was why he was putting on weight. Back in the old station in Eglinton Street he used to bound up the stairs and down again but then he was playing football in these days. He looked at his reflection in the mirror inside the lift and patted down his hair, but it wouldn't stay down. It had gone wild these past few years and had developed this wiry look that would never be thick again, no matter how many sprays he put on it at night. He pulled in his stomach but it still stuck out. He wanted to lose weight this summer. He'd promised himself and Mary that he'd be fitter by the time the holidays came so that he wouldn't look the way he looked last year. It's bad enough being white but being white and fat, well that was another thing. The lift door opened, just seconds after he had gotten in. First floor. Last door on the right. He walked down, nodded at the secretary. He knew what the Super wanted him for. At least this time, there wouldn't be any humiliation in front of the others, even though Miss Motormouth there would have it around the place in no time.

Somebody had broken half his nameplate off the door so now it read SuperQuigley like in Superman. Quigley had blamed some gurrier who had been in for questioning, but everyone knew it was Fogarty who did it. He laughed at his handiwork and then knocked on the door.
'Come in.'
'You wanted to see me, sir?'
'Garda Fogarty, sit down.'
'Thank you, sir.'
'I'll get straight to the point. I'm not happy with certain aspects of your work...'
'In what way, sir?'
'Let me finish. I have...'
'Sorry, sir.'
'I have been monitoring the situation since the incident with the fire extinguisher and things have not improved very much...'

Nightmusic

Fogarty sat back in the chair and let the Super rabbit on. He knew what was bugging him. He knew there were others in the Communications Room who had squealed on him and let it out about his language on the radios. He knew too that the Super was pissed off at him for the way he let massive queues build up at the front desk. Fogarty knew everyone and what car they drove and so he'd engage people in conversation. It was only being civil, after all.

'...I don't like the public in the building for longer than necessary. When they are on our premises, we are responsible and many of our visitors are less than desirable characters, so holding them up talking rubbish is not the proper way of dealing with the public.'

'I've given you a stint in the Communications Room in the hope that you would work out, but I'm afraid it has not been successful. The unsavoury language out of you on our radio waves the other night was disgraceful. I will not allow it and I will not preside over such shoddy work practises...'

Fogarty wanted to scratch his balls badly.
Genuinely.
But he knew if he did, it'd go down badly,
He also wanted to tell the Super to fuck off badly.
Genuinely.
But that would go down badly as well, so he said nought and hoped the itch would go away.
And the Super.
He knew too that the Super was under pressure himself, as he badly wanted to be Chief Super and knew that he was being monitored from above and that he'd been getting calls from Phoenix Park all summer every time some eejit went on the radio and rightly said that the city was gone to fuck regarding violence.
At the start of the summer he'd told them that he wanted to cool things considerably over July and August. He knew that the Arts Festival and the Races brought headers to town and he was determined to keep a lid on things. He'd been told that he could not have any more officers and that if he needed help he could bring them in from Tuam and Headford and Ballinasloe. And then it'd be his fault if some of those gurriers attacked some elderly folk living in an isolated area while the local Gardai were in Galway policing racegoers who had more money than sense. The Super would love if it was September again. But it was still

Nightmusic

July. Sometimes Fogarty felt sorry for the Super, even though he could never tell why. SuperQuigley was a sincere enough kind of bloke but he had gotten this far and he didn't really didn't want to fuck it up now. Fogarty on the other hand was still a Guard and it seemed would always be a Guard now. He'd had no time for exams after he rammed the first few. After that, he just lost the bottle every time he went in, so now this was his lot and he'd have to accept it. But he still had his Scott medal and his Corporation citation for bravery and they couldn't take those away from him. What bugged him most of all was that the Super had never visited him when he was in hospital for those tests after the syringe attack, that he had never asked how he was, that he had never asked how Mary was, or the kids and how his fuckin' nerves were after it all. He didn't see any of that but yet he had time to monitor everything else. Well, monitor this, he thought as he went to scratch the itch. But he stopped.

'..And so I am left with little choice at this stage but to place you back on the street on patrol duties and away from the station where your behaviour has led to a lessening of morale and brought a general feeling of ridicule. You will resume street duties on Thursday week and we'll...'
Gosh the itch was really bad now. He had to scratch, so he did, grabbing his crotch and forcefully rooting into it with his fingers.
The Super stopped and looked and then pointed at Fogarty's crotch.
'...and that's more of it. That kind of lack of respect for authority. You have no sense of decorum. No wonder you never, ah, never mind.'
'But sir, that...'
'But sir what? You have an excuse for everything. An excuse for your behaviour. I know you're the funny man in the locker room. I know you've no time for the kind of ideas I'm trying to introduce around here, but could you at least keep those fucking opinions to yourself?'
Fogarty sat back in the chair letting go of his crotch. It was the first time he'd heard the Super swear and he thought he should swear more often because he did it beautifully. Pronouncing every syllable of the word fuuuuuuccccckkkkiiiinnngg. No ordinary fuckin' and blinding for SuperQuigley.

When he got home he told Mary that he'd had a row with the Super and that he requested to be put back on patrol. He knew he couldn't tell her the truth. She'd kill him, she would, with her brown eyes and dark hair back in a ponytail and her shrill teacher's voice, well able to shout him down in any row. They'd sat back a year earlier and drank a bottle of cheap wine to celebrate how well both of their careers were going, that he was settling in well now under Quigley and that she had gotten the Transition Year job she wanted, the one where her imagination and creativity would be put to far better use than they were when she was only teaching Irish and Geography and organising the Christmas play. He loved Mary but he knew that if she knew what a fuck-up he was making of his career in Galway, she'd never forgive him. She had told him to watch his mouth and take it easy with the jokes, but she didn't really understand what it was like to go in here night after night not knowing what sort of mad fucker was going to come at ya with a syringe.

He had a bath, washed himself well and snuggled up behind her in the bed and kept his thoughts to himself. She rolled him over and put her head on his chest and hugged her Garda, the man who's so good that he's mastered everything below in the station.

But as he lay there staring at the ceiling once she'd fallen asleep, he was glad he hadn't said anything to the Super about what he thought about the suicides. The Super would probably laugh at him if he brought in Lord Lucan, never mind a load of makey-uppy bollocks of a suspicion he had.

* * * *

Nightmusic

Malachy couldn't believe how easy it was.
When he drove up Bishop O'Donnell Road, towards the new roundabout and out towards the Prom, he hadn't expected to see one that soon.
But he did.
They were arguing the first time he drove past and when he went by a few minutes later, they were still at it. Four of them. Three in one group all in their late teens, all with big tits, and another, with brown hair and bright pink trousers moving away from them, telling them they were a shower of cunts and that she didn't want anything to do with them.
He drove by, slowly at first and then quickening the pace. Can't be too obvious, you see. He loved fishing at this hour of the night because the fish are less sharp and vulnerable. He lowered the window the next time he passed and saw that it was a real row. They were all holding bottles of some white drink, probably Smirnoff or something like that. As he passed the fourth time, she looked at the van and straight at him, but continued to bollock the companions. He knew then that she'd do. Fate had decreed it. She had given him the look. He drove by down the hill and pulled into the dark area where one block of the Rahoon flats used to be.

He had tried to get a younger one the year before out past Spiddal. About eight or nine, she was, with sort of a dress like you'd wear at dancing class, although not as expensive. He asked her directions and offered her sweets. He thought afterwards how corny the sweets thing was, but it seemed like a good idea at the time. And what's the point asking them the way to Rosmuc or anything anyway, what the fuck do they know? Sweets, they know. Directions, they don't. Go for their basic instincts. He looked in her eyes through the open door of the van and saw that for a split second she was going to get in, but she didn't. She took off down the road like a fuckin' hare and across some fields. He laughed later when he heard the description of his van on the radio. The stupid kid had all the colours wrong and even had a few others in the van with him. And from the voice of the Guard he could tell that they probably didn't believe her anyway.
But he didn't want kids, even though he'd gone back again and tried others. They ran away as well. They did nothing for him so there was no point taking a risk. It's too dangerous and he didn't fancy finishing them anyway. With a kid on your hands, you're stuck with it. That's

why all those English bastards get caught eventually. They see a kid, act on instinct and never think of what to do afterwards. But he, Malachy, is different. He sees further than the end of his, ya know. He knows that there is a beginning, a middle and an end to every fishing trip and that when every fish has been cleaned and gutted, there's nothing left for anyone, but the cat.

So no more kids.

After a few more minutes parked there in the darkness, he headed back up the road again. They were still at it. She was about eighteen or nineteen and she was still giving her friends a right bollocking. He lowered the window and watched her while pulling in on the roadside.

She'd do what she fuckin' liked, he heard her say before she stormed off down the hill towards the new hotel at the junction of the Rahoon cemetery road. She crossed over to head for the gap which brought her through the fields to the housing estate, but she took her time. Time enough for him to drive around the edge of the estate and park in the trees, before getting out and making his way into the woods. It was well after 2 a.m. now and there was no-one around. He was amazed how soon he saw her come through the field, and make for the gap leading to the path to the estate. He felt his heart beating, his excitement growing. She had lit a cigarette by this stage and had stopped by the edge of the woods to finish it before she got home. She was fumbling in her handbag for something as she sat on a tree stump and took another long drag of the fag. He moved through the grass with speed and little sound, and came through the clearing and into the darkness. He could see the light of the fag glowing brightly with every drag and he decided to wait until it next grew red,
And when it did, it was for the last time, as the butt flew upwards when she fell backwards, his right hand sticking the broad cellophane across the bottom of her face and then her mouth. She fell to the ground and started to struggle. Fuckin' bitch was kicking like hell, and even though her mouth was taped, there was still a moan coming through and she was flailing, so he threw her down on her chest and grabbed her arms, and put the tape around them and then kneeling on the back of her thighs, he grabbed her ankles and placed them so that both shin bones were bound together.

Nightmusic

He could feel her heartbeat accelerating as her muffled cries continued and then he saw that the tape was over her nose and that she was suffocating, so he grabbed the tape and pulled it down to expose her nostrils. She snorted as he turned her around and then she passed out. He lifted her, checking to make sure nothing was left on the pathway. Got through the bushes and to the back of the van where he had the back door ajar. He flicked it open with his heel and bundled her inside, strapping her torso to the wall inside with brown buckled strap that was used to hold the fishboxes for the mackerel. These straps were handy. He remembered how another one had rolled around in the van when he was heading out the coast road past Barna and she hit her head on the sledge hammer and tools in the bag and the place was covered with blood. But that was only the once and now he didn't drive as fast, but that fuckin' road is desperate anyway. I must tell the county councillor, he thought as he went past the prom at Furbo, and turned onto the sideroad that led to the farm and the shed and the cellar.

Mother always said he was a bit of a ditherer.
And 'twas true for her.
He didn't know whether to toss off while the girl was still there or wait until he got back later and looked at the Polaroids.
But it wasn't something you could ask Mother about.
He had to free some of the tape to open her clothing, and her top took some dragging, but he left her mouth and her eyes covered and proceeded gently, with the greatest of care, the camera flashing harshly as he moved around, then closer and closer, taking everything but her face, nothing that could be identified in the photos, a pile of which grew on the shelf.
He took a dozen and then tossed off in the semi-light, with little sound in the room but the swish of his sleeve and the whimpering and breathing of Patrice Nolan as she lay on the slab, her clothes around her ankles, and her breasts exposed to the yellow light.

He hated the feeling immediately after he had come. Up until then, everything had seemed worthwhile, but now even the pictures seemed useless. He knew that as soon as he wiped himself, the guilt would set in and the whole point of taking her would be fucking gone. He hated having to return the fish to the sea afterwards as he felt less sharp after he had tossed off. Beforehand, he was alert to everything, but the brief

Nightmusic

feeling of pleasure and its subsequent release stole that level of concentration from him.

He knew that it was still not too late to let her go. But that's how the others had gotten caught and he wasn't like the others. So he played some Mozart, the *Piano Concerto No. 21*, the *Elvira Madigan* one. And that sort of relaxed him again, while charging him at the same time. It had the danger to make ya sleepy, but he wouldn't let it. At the sound of the music, the girl on the slab started to whimper a bit more.

He washed his hands in the sink in the corner and then carefully, he dressed her again, running the tip of his finger along her stomach as he said goodbye to her flat heaving stomach. Time to go time.

You can never be too sure about these things. No point delaying. What's the Latin line they have when they catch you? Habeas corpus. Something to to do with the body. Whatever it meant, if ya got rid of the body, the fuckers were less likely to get ya. And anyway, there was a smell in the shed, as she'd pissed on the slab. But they all did that.

It was after 4 a.m. when the van left the shed and trundled down the road to the boat. That's the dying hour. The nurse from the hospital had told him that, the time the woman down the road had died. It's when the body is most relaxed and lacking in the energy to stay on living, she had said. But this one wasn't relaxed. Her legs kicked again in the back of the van at the shore. Across the bay he could see some lights on, across in Ballyvaughan or at *Black Head*. The lights of a car made their way along the cliff, as he lowered her into the boat, and then rowed silently for about 20 minutes until he was out far enough. He left the fishing rods on the floor. He brought them in case anyone asked him what he was at, and he'd say he was out dipping feathers for cod. He rowed for Shantalla once, but just the once because Mother said that rowing was only for those in the colleges who would have jobs to walk into and not for dockboys who had mothers to look after.

She sighed again and gave a sort of moan. He grabbed her by the hair and held her over until she was facing the water and then he pushed the head downwards and hummed *Galway Bay*. Just 30 seconds or so, until he got to the sun rising over Claddagh bit. That should be enough. Bubbles came in the water. He heard the first few but then the humming

Nightmusic

drummed out the next few, and the next, until there were none. He lifted her head back in but there was still some life there, so he gave her another verse. One for the road, you might say, and then when all life had disappeared from her body, he took off the tapes, first from the eyes, then from the mouth and then the legs and arms before lifting her into the water and holding her head just below the surface. Then he let Patrice Nolan slip into the darkness of the bay, before he headed for home and some food.

'There can be no question, my dear Watson, of the value of exercise before breakfast.'

* * * *

The clock rang out five.

Delia Lee turned in her sleep.

She had heard each of the previous six rings of the clock. It was a dreadful nuisance sometimes, comforting during the day, but at night, there was a sense of time creeping about it. Every tick tock in the dark felt longer.

Downstairs, the mug with two heaped spoonfuls of cocoa powder stood beside the kettle where Mother had placed it seven hours earlier. But the kettle was cold again now and would have to be boiled up. She wasn't sure if he had come in or not. Sometimes, when he was working late, he came in, crept up the stairs and into his own room without peeking in at all. Then other nights, he'd bring up the supper to her.

She tried to right herself over in the bed, but the sharp pain flew up her hip. The hip where the bone was broken after she fell over the cat. It was the second time this year that she had fallen over the cat and on neither occasion had she seen the animal. In fact, she never knew there was a cat around the house for ages, but there must be, because Malachy had seen the whole thing and he had warned her on both times just as she fell. He saw the cat, so there must be a cat. Probably one he lets in late at night off the street for a feed. A stray from up Spires Garden or that way. And now she had a constant reminder of the pain, but maybe not for very long more. Maybe, she would soon have a new hip and the pain would be gone.

She had wanted to get Dr. O'Malley up to have a look at it, but Malachy said there was no need for anything like that and he had bandaged her himself, but the pain was still there and eventually the doctor came and

Nightmusic

now she was on the list for the hip job, but she'd read in the *Tribune* that she could be waiting for five years. The *Tribune* was great for waiting list stories. It was full of them, a different one every week. She had been on the list for three months now and it could be another while before she gets the letter from Merlin Park. She hadn't been in Merlin for some years now. She didn't like it there, it was a depressing place. Malachy had said that it was a like a fuckin' prison camp. He was dreadfully coarse these days, but she put it down to the lads he was working with. They swore and drank and gambled and it was inevitable, some of it would rub off on him. It was a good job Paddy wasn't here. He'd have stopped him swearing even though he swore a lot himself, especially when he got mad at the McGintys and threw things around.

She loved it when he finished his work early and when he'd come in and tell her all that was happening down at the Claddagh and how it had changed an awful lot. And how he'd seen Nora Kennedy down town, you know Nora who helped deliver me and then if she fell asleep by the fire, he'd carry her up the stairs because he was strong like that and put her in her bed and tuck her in. Nora was always asking for her; she had been her and Paddy's best friend when they got married but she hadn't called around much lately. Malachy didn't like visitors to the house. He told her they were only after her money. She knew she didn't have much, but there was no telling him. Nora had told her that she called a few times and Malachy had said that Mother was gone up to her sister's place in Tuam, but she wasn't. Maybe he was just protecting her, she thought.

But tonight, he was working late. Maybe he was even called out on an emergency, with the Guards or the lifeboat. He loved doing that sort of work, helping in rescues and being in the middle of the action. There was no sign of him by 10 o'clock, so she left the cocoa there for him and a plate of digestives, so he wouldn't go to bed on an empty stomach, the poor soul.
She turned in the bed and winced again.
It had taken her an age to get up the stairs tonight. She had seen in one of those Sunday magazines that there was a chair lift you could get up the side of the stairs, but Malachy said that knowing her, she'd probably fall off the bloody thing and then where would she be. And besides, it

Nightmusic

would probably cost thousands. It'd be cheaper to build a bungalow, he had told her.

The clock struck the half hour. And another chill went down her spine, meeting the pain coming up her hip and hitting her in the midriff somewhere. When she was a child, she hated the thought of being old and alone at night with no-one to hear her if she cried out. The night is so unforgiving. It belongs to different creatures, young lively people who have fun or who rob and attack old people. It is not a time for the old. Darkness makes them feel older, and creeps up on them like a blanket of black dust descending upon their ailing lungs.

Just after a quarter to six, she heard the latch go on the door downstairs and she lifted her head off the pillow until she knew for sure it was him. She was always happy when her family were in for the night. Her family of one. And now they were. She heard the whistle of the kettle as it soared into action and the clink of the plate as he ate the biscuits, before he made the climb up the stairs and into his room at the back, his good deed done for the day.

* * * *

Nightmusic

Her friends were of little help.
They had already been hauled into Mill St. by Patrice Nolan's father, Paddy. They had been with her last. They were the ones she'd gone to town with and now a day and a half later, there was still no sign of her. He told them to wait in the car 'cos he wasn't finished with them.

'Calm down, Mr. Nolan. She might have gone off on the train or something. Had she any money with her?' asked the young Garda at the desk.
'£20 I gave her for going out. That's all. She's working so she might have had her own money.'
'I see.'
'Listen here. My daughter went out to a disco two nights ago and has not come home.'
'Has she done this before?'
'Once. Last year. She went to a sleep over party and got drunk. But she came back the following day. And her friends, who were supposed to be fuckin' looking after her are out in the car. They haven't seen her either.'
'Bring them in.'

They didn't make much sense either. They didn't want to say that Patrice had been banging a fella who worked in the post office in town. A sorter or a postman. One of those jobs. He'd been sorting her anyway. All deliveries round the back and that sort of stuff.
Not here in front of her father.
No, they couldn't say that.
He had stopped her going to the Debs the year before that, so imagine the reaction he'd have had if he knew she was getting stamped by a postman. He'd have freaked, so they had to make up their own story about the row. But there were two or three of them and the Chinese Whispers theory ensured the story fell apart in pissing time. Now Paddy Nolan was really fuming. He knew something was up. SuperQuigley knew something was up to. He wasn't going to have a member of the public carrying out his own interrogation in his station, so he brought him up to a room upstairs and told Garda Sheehan to fill out the forms and get the necessary details. His own lads would find out the truth from the girls.
Which they did in no time.

Nightmusic

The postman was only getting out of bed when the squad car containing Fogarty and Sheehan pulled up at his house. Garda Noel Fogarty knew the postman was a randy fucker who'd get up on the crack of dawn, so denying he knew Patrice was a waste of time.
'Noel...' he said when he came to the door, a fag in his hand.
'Don't Noel me now. It's Garda Fogarty to you.'
They told him why they were there and he started to yap.
'Ya know how it is. I met her a few times, but I never touched her. Well, ya know, but she told me she's eighteen.'
'That's OK, she is,' said Fogarty, 'but that still doesn't make it right.'
'Well, what did she say? I never, like. She was on for it...'
'Nothing, she's said nothing. That's the problem, she hasn't been home since the night before last. When did you see her last?'
'Not for a week or so. OK, four days ago.'
The postman was squirming on his own doorstep. Inside, Fogarty could see his wife moving around with some kids.
'So tell us more. The more ya talk, the more ya say. How long has this been going on?'
'I only rode her twice. I swear to fuck. There was nothing else.'
'The postman only knocks twice, does he?' said Fogarty, but the Postman wasn't laughing.
His wife was wondering what the story was.
She came to the door.
'Is there anything wrong, love?'
'No, Sheila, go back in. It's one of the fellas at work. He's up to something.' She went back into the kitchen.
'You're an awful fucker, Reilly, hopping on young ones.'
'Ssssh, yeah, I know, but jaysus don't tell Sheila.'
'So I take it she's not in this house then?'
'Fuck, no. I swear lads, I haven't seen her since Monday. I was supposed to see her the other night, but she didn't arrive.'
'Ya know Paddy Nolan would kill ya if he found out ya were ridin' his daughter.'
'I know, I know. He was a hard enough chaw when he was playing for Hibs in the seventies.'
'Right, if she gets in touch with ya, let me know immediately and if I hear you've been holding out on me, it'll be more than Sheila and Paddy Nolan who'll be gunnin' for ya.'
Fogarty poked him in the groin with the aerial of the radio.

'And keep that beast tied up at home.'

Paddy Nolan went on the Keith Finnegan show on Galway Bay fm the following morning. He had gotten wind that there was a boyfriend somewhere and so he appealed to Patrice to come home.
He broke down midway through his sentence but Keith Finnegan went into an ad break to give him a chance to compose himself which he did just as the break ended.
'Patrice luv, if you're out there, come home. I don't mind what ya have done. Your mammy and I love ya. Just get to a phone and ring us. And if there is anyone out there who might have seen her, tell her it doesn't matter what she's up to, just give a ring on the number to put our minds at rest. Patrice, everyone who loves ya is worried, so get in touch.'

The frail hand went over and switched off the radio.
Mother loved her radio, Especially the one he got her with the preset buttons which meant you didn't have to be moving the dial this way and that. Now she could get Galway Bay fm in the morning for the news and the deaths, and get *Liveline* in the afternoon and the soft music from Lyric in the evening and back to Galway Bay fm again for more deaths in the evening.
'That's another girl that they're looking for. Too much money they have nowadays. When I was young there was nowhere to go to, but now you can fly away or get a train and be in England in a few hours or so. Nora Kennedy was telling me a few years ago that she saw a bus down in Eyre Square and it had London on it. You can get a bus straight to London now from Galway. The furthest in our time was Dublin. It's the bright lights that attract them, foolish young amadans.'
Malachy didn't pay any heed to her. He just continued to read his Independent, which he knew drove her daft.
She leaned over and took a slice of bread out of the bag.
'Sounds like a pretty girl, so she does.'
'Yeah,' grunted Malachy across the table.
She was pretty all right. He could feel the stir in his trousers to testify to it. And when he put his cup to his mouth, he could still smell the oh so sweet perfume that she must have plastered all over herself and inside that maroon bra.

* * * *

Nightmusic

When Fogarty came through the door, he heard the sniffling.
'What's wrong, luv?'
Mary ran to him and threw her arms around him.
'What is it? Is it the kids?'
'No, no. Sorry, maybe I'm being a bit silly. It's that Nolan girl. I knew her. I taught her. She was in one of my classes. Remember the play we did, *Snow White*? She was in that when she was in First Year. Lovely kid. Lovely kid. Any word on her, Noel?'
'No, nothing, she's just missing still. She could be anywhere. Maybe she ran off or something.'
'But that's sad, don't ya think? Noel, she was a lovely kid when she was younger. She was the sweetest one in the drama classes and always dreamed of playing the princess. She was Snow White in that play and she was brilliant in it.'
'Don't be worrying, Mary luv. Kids do things like this. She'll turn up in London or something.'
'It's so sad, though. I really thought she'd make it and go to University or something. That class I took for that play were so good. They were all lovely kids and I'd meet them in town and they'd go out of their way to say 'Hello, Mrs. Fogarty' and almost run up to you to get some greeting in return, but now, when I meet them, they've lost that warmth. They're bigger and colder and just mutter an embarrassed hello at ya if ya talk to them.'
'That's teenagers, Mary. Sure it'll happen to your own two here...'
'I know, but it makes me wonder about the point of the job at all, if all we're doing is delaying their transformation into cold, dour teenagers. They seem to be contaminated by their peers.'
'That's just part of growing up...'
'I don't know, I don't think we did the same. I don't think we became so grown up so quickly. These kids showed great promise. Take Patrice, I brought them on a trip to see the Uni one day and they were all saying how they'd like to go there and get mortar boards on their heads, but now many of them are pushing prams around and stuck in the lives their young mothers had. It's just such a shame and it seems to be only the city girls who are turning this way. The country ones are fine, I suppose they're not subjected to the same problems.'
'Sure it's the same for me in the station. We see people at their worst, their most vulnerable, but it doesn't mean that we give up...'
'No, I'm not going to give up, it just pisses me off now and again that it

could be all pointless. Is what you're doing pointless? You and the other guards are down there every night and still there is crime. It never gets better.'

'All we can do is hold it at bay, luv. That's all we can do.'

He took her face and kissed it, tasted the salty taste of the tears running down her cheeks.

'Will ya try and make the city a better place for our two, luv?' she said. 'They're so young and innocent now, but they'll get contaminated by it, if it gets out of hand.'

'I promise,' he said and then he hugged her so tight that she had to burst out laughing to stop him from breaking her back. He felt sad too, but decided not to tell Mary about the postman jumping young Patrice.

It'd break her heart altogether if she thought Snow White's Prince Charming rode a Post office bike instead of a golden carriage.

* * * *

Nightmusic

The radio was blaring in the newsroom when the Chief came in and tapped Terry on the ear.
'One headline I allow ya to make up for me on your computer and ya manage to fuck it up.'
'What, Chief?'
'The story about the stolen car being located in the woods.'
'Yes.'
Since when do inanimate objects have the power of locating things?'
'Sorry Chief, I'm not with ya.'
Look at the fucking headline.
STOLEN CAR FOUND BY TREES.
'Do trees now go around finding cars, do they? Did they ring the guards and say, 'We found this and we'd like to report it?' Think, man, think, before ya use your ink.'
He threw the sheet down and went out the door.

Just after the Chief had left, Aoife nodded to Morley to come outside. She left before him and headed down town. He met her in the hotel a few minutes later and when he got there, she had a cappuccino ordered for him.
'Cappuccino. Far from fuckin' cappuccinos I was reared.'
'Shut up and drink up.'
'What d'ya want?'
'That's a nice way to start. No, I've a message for ya. A cousin of mine, a guard in Galway. He's seen your stuff in the nationals and he wants to talk to ya.'
'Is he pissed off at me or what?'
'No, he's not. He just wants to talk.'
'Shag off. Guards never just want to talk. Doesn't work for the revenue commissioners, does he?'
'No. He reckons he has a bit of a story for ya and he needs some help.'
'Right. I hate when people tell me they have stories for me. They usually turn out to be shite.'
'Well, will ya meet him?'
'Right.'
'I'll tell him, so.'
'And why do you not want to do it, this story.?'
'He asked for you.'
'Even more suspicious.'

Nightmusic

'I'm only passing on a message. Maybe he wants you to write his memoirs,' she said, taking a drag on her fag.
'OK, I'll meet him. In Galway.'

* * * *

Davy Morley loved the cloak and dagger stuff. Meeting strangers in dark corners for the job. The kind of stuff he'd dreamed about when he watched films like *All the President's Men* and *The Parallax View*. Deep Throat and all that.
He chose to meet Garda Fogarty in Bar Cuba on Prospect Hill because it was full of nooks and crannies where you could hide away and have a discreet chat, an affair, a read, a fag, a decent feed, or a drink, and no-one would bother you. Unless you wanted to be bothered there among the posters of Che Guevara and beautiful Havana women running down streets carrying flags.
He went to the bar where John took his order of a Brandy and Coke.
'Working the weekend?' asked John.
'Yeah, as always. Matches. Junior Intermediate B Finals.'
'Any good?'
'Shite of a standard only third choice bogball players could achieve.'
Morley hated GAA. And the officials and a lot of the followers too, and so he took a particular pleasure in writing stuff that had them foaming at the mouth. This he did regularly, much to the embarrassment of the sports editor at the *Chronicle* who had been cultivating GAA relationships for forty years and who'd call him in on an almost monthly basis to tell him that such and such a thing could not be said as it was conflicting with the ethos of the GAA.
'Bring it down to ya,' said John.

Morley found one of those dark corners from where you could see the door but not be seen. He hated meeting Guards in these one to one situations. You'd never know what they really wanted. He remembered once how he'd written some story in the *Chronicle* and two detectives called around to his house the following Saturday morning and asked him where he got his information. On a Saturday fuckin' morning at 9 o' clock. He had little doubt but it was a warning to stop writing that shite in the paper because it was making them look bad. When he told the Chief, he went daft. He wanted to ring the local Superintendent to

Nightmusic

complain about harassment of his reporter's democratic rights, but he decided against it. The Gardai were needed for the scribbling job so his reporter's democratic rights could take a kicking now and again.

Morley didn't know what Noel Fogarty looked like. But he prided himself on spotting Guards a mile off. It's the innate curiosity and that 'I know where you live' expression they always carry that gave it away. He was starving, so he ordered chicken quesadillas, with extra chilli. And fries on the side. And another drink.

Fogarty was 15 minutes late. He came in the door and spent an age looking around. He hadn't been in here before. Christ, it was dark and the music, sort of South American, kind of dago music, the kind you'd hear in some fuckin' place like Cuba, the country that is, not the bar. It was like non-stop fuckin' Gypsy Kings. John was over to serve him like a flash and see what he could get him, but Fogarty wasn't ordering anything yet and no he wasn't going to give John any idea of what the fuck he wanted. He continued looking around until his eyes met with Morley's. Spotting that Morley already had a drink, he called back John and ordered one for himself and made his way over to the table.
'David Morley, is it?'
'Yeah, Noel Fogarty, is it?'
He nodded.
'It's fuckin' dark in here, isn't it?' he said, squinting down at Morley.
'Well, I could have had a seat for us in the front window of News At Ten, but I thought you wanted this to be discreet.'
'Discreet. Yeah, discreet is good.'
John brought down Morley's food and Fogarty's pint of Harp and left the yellow docket in the centre of the table. For them to fight over. No one went for it.
Fogarty looked down at the quesadillas.
'What the fuck is that?' he asked, pointing his finger at the plate.
'Chicken quesadillas. A Cuban chicken dish.'
'Fuck me, I'd say it's hot.'
Yeah, it is. Anyway, Aoife told me you had something to ask me.'
'How is she?' asked Fogarty.
'She's great.'
'Grand girl. Still got the Opel?'
'I think so.'

Nightmusic

'Mighty fuckin' car that. 'Twas a steal.'
'Yeah. I'd say that.'
'How are things out in the sticks? Are the fuckin' knackers still batin' the shite out o' wan another with slash-hooks? It's part of what they are, ya know. Part of their culture. Me hole, it is.'
He sipped his Harp.
'Oh, yeah, sure the court clerks would be out of a job if it weren't for them.' said Morley.
'And the *Chronicle* would be a lot thinner,' laughed Fogarty, wiping the froth off his lips.
'Aye.'
He was a lot heavier than Morley had expected. And tougher looking. Today he wore jeans and a fleece-sweatshirt with the words 'Just Do It' emblazoned across the front. Morley reckoned that those words were often uttered by Fogarty to a "fuckin' knacker" who dared to cross him. He could feel the Garda's eyes scan him up and down as if searching for some flaw.
'So, have ya a story for me or what is it I can do for ya?'
Fogarty sat back in the chair and then leaned forward before speaking.
'I think we can do something for each other.'
He stopped and waited for a response, but Morley had a mouthful of quesadillas, so he said nothing.
'I need to know who I'm dealing with, though. I can't talk to just any prick. 'Jesus, if any of the lads see me coming into trendy places like this, I'll get a reputation,' said Fogarty looking around.
'Stall on, it's grand.'
He slurped the Harp.
Morley sipped the brandy and coke.
'I heard about some of the stuff you write, good stuff and that's unusual for a reporter in these parts. Most of them are happy to sit around on their holes and write about hurling and waste management plans and shite like that and protect their own arses. I've been told you don't give a shite but that you're careful.'
Morley didn't know where this was leading, but it was praise and it was coming from a Garda.
'I've pissed off a few Guards too.'
'I know. They came out to your house. Two suits. From Tuam, and that takes some sort of balls on your behalf. That's why I asked Aoife if I could meet ya and tell you what I have in mind.'

Nightmusic

'Right, shoot.'

'I might have a story which could benefit both you and me. However, without going into things, there are too many obstacles in my path at the moment below in the station. I've been taken from behind everywhere I go, if ya know what I mean, so I need some help on it.'

'But where do I come into this?'

'I might be able to give you some information on something I've been looking at. It's a solo run, this. No one else on the flanks. But I can only do so much, you'll have to do a fair bit as well. Ask the difficult questions like.'

'So what's the story?'

'That's the thing. I'm still working it out in my own head.'

'Fuck,' thought Morley, a Garda working something out in his head. Is this a waste of time or not?

'No, it's like that. I just need to have a contact in the media. Most of the others down there have one, but what they're feeding ye is bullshit. The best stuff stays hidden. If I were to make some of this available to ya in dribs and drabs, you might be able to ask questions and make someone look a bit stupid.'

'Who is this someone? Is it a vendetta ya have? I don't want to be caught up in a guard sandwich.'

'No, you'll find out soon enough. Can I be fuckin' straight with ya, David? I'm 46 years of age and still just a Guard. Now in Garda terms, that's fuckin' shockin', but I've given a lot to the force and I don't think it's given me back the same commitment...'

Morley thought about how the fuck he got messed up in this. He'd kill Aoife when he got back for landing him with her loony Garda cousin obviously experiencing some sort of breakdown, but he nodded anyway and let Fogarty ramble on.

'Now, don't get me wrong. I love being a guard, but it has fucked me up rightly in the last few years. Ya see, I got stabbed with a syringe and I thought I might be HIV positive. I sweated through my hole for three months and even when I got the all clear, I used to get nightmares about it. I'd see myself in the mirror and I'd look like Rock Hudson.'

'That's not bad. Ya could have been Doris Day,' said Morley but he instantly regretted it.

'No, I mean when Hudson was fuckin' dying. I was like a bag o' weasels all the time and I ... I don't know if ya heard about this, but I dropped a fire extinguisher on a prisoner's foot during an interrogation.'

'Dropped?'
'Well, I, I fuckin' threw it at him, but he had just insulted one of the ban Gardai, said she had no tits at all.'
'How the fuck did he say that?'
'She asked him a question about why he was stalking a woman and he said what the fuck would she know about love when she had no tits at all.'
Morley laughed.
'It was funny, but you should have seen him hop when the extinguisher fell. It scared the shite out of him. After that he was more cooperative, but the Super heard about it below and chewed the arse off me, so I've been on the slippery slope ever since.'
'So where do I come in and what's the next step?'
'Sit tight. I'll be in touch with ya in a few weeks and I'll let ya know what's happening. I have a plan.'
'A cunning plan, is it?'
'Yeah, that's what it is. A cunning plan. Have ya a mobile number?'
Morley said he had and handed it over.
'And yourself.'
'I'll give ya that later. When I can trust ya. If you get a story, it can't be connected to me at all, so no calls for me to my mobile, the office or at home. The fuckers check phone records so we can't say anything.'
'What fuckers?'
'The heads below.'

And then he was gone, with a promise to be in touch. He had to get back on duty and some young wan was missing.
He went too without paying John for his drink, so Morley had to cough for all the drinks and the quesadillas.
And he was still fuck all the wiser about the point of the whole meeting.

* * * *

Nightmusic

Peadar O Fatharta was in no mood for doing any work today, but the way his head felt, he just wanted to get away from land, crawl into a boat and get out and do the cages. That way, Niamh couldn't get on to him again.
She'd been like a bear, the way she was going on, ringing his mobile and sending text messages with bollocks spelt wrong on them.
Fuck her anyway. It's not as if he was married to her or anything.
He could talk to whoever he liked and dance with whoever he liked, and as long as she didn't find out, he could throw his leg over whoever he liked. But she had found out and most likely from Maire Ni Riain who ran the new hostel in Kilronan who probably watched him slip in with the Dutch backpacker, take the place of her rucksack and make the beast with two backs with Heidi Van rentals or whatever the fuck her name was.
'Ol agus dick. Ol agus dick. And what about Aids?' Niamh had said to him
'Aids, me hole,' he told her.
And she'd said 'Yeah, exactly.'
There's no Aids on Aran and surely today wouldn't be the day Aids Came to Aran. The Day Aids Came To Aran. That'd make a great name for a Waterboys tune.
'Niamh, cop on will ya? You're losing the fuckin' plot here,' he pleaded with her, but she wasn't having any of it.
'You should have it cut off you, Peadar Beag.'
She hung up.
He hated being called Peadar Beag. Even if his father was Peadar Mór. He was Peadar Mór for a reason. He was a big greasy fat fucker who everyone knew as Peadar Mor. Peadar Beag wasn't beag at all. He was average, but still, the name stuck on him, but Niamh only used it when she was really angry, and I suppose missing a date and staying out all night shagging a Dutch bird was one of those little things that made her hate him.
'I love you too,' he said to the dead line. And that's why his head hurt.

So he decided to go and check the cages. At least the lobster wouldn't try to get their claws into him like she had. There was something nice about early morning on Aran, as the tourists hadn't staggered down from the B&Bs, and the first boats and planes weren't due in for another while yet. Consequently, he took a piss behind the rock beside the boat,

Nightmusic

and watched a rabbit scurry across a field.
'Hurry home, ya little fucker. Ya can screw who ya like and no one bothers ya,' he said.

He walked gingerly to the shore. She'd given him a right going over all right, the Dutch one, hopping up and down and gripping her ankles around his legs so hard he thought his calves were going to burst.
He pushed the boat out and then hopped in, guiding its nose past the rocks with the one oar there was. Peadar Mór had sat on the other one and made shit of it. He took out his mobile and thought about ringing Kevin in Rossaveal to tell him about the Dutch bird and tell him that what she couldn't do wasn't worth bothering about. But the credit on the mobile was low, so there was no point and he left it on the seat and rowed slowly with an oar in one hand and a floorboard from the boat in the other. It only took him a minute to get to the cages.
Peadar Mor would be surprised that he did them willingly this morning, but today the cages were sort of therapeutic, a sort of natural Alka Seltzer. He leaned over and dragged at the thick cables that secured them. A quick gawk and then home for the fry and crawl into the bed for the morning. He looked around the island. 'Twas too early to be up on Inis Mór. He pulled the cable again, but there was no give at all.
He pulled again, this time leaving down the oar. Still no give. Fuck, his arms couldn't be this tired. His balls were red raw but his arms, well they should be OK, but the more he pulled, the more tension was on the rope.
... and the more he pulled, the clearer into view came the redness from beneath the water
... and the more he pulled, the more of the pink trousers came into view
... and the more he pulled, the more he saw of the eaten face of what he presumed was a young girl, a lobster clinging onto her head, one claw in the hole where her left eye should have been.
He let go of the cables and let the lot splash back into the water.

The lifeboat chief in Kilronan rang the guards in Rossaveal who rang Salthill who told Mill Street and before long, the news was out that a body had been found washed up on Inis Mor.
'The body as yet unidentified is believed to be that of a young woman, but no formal identification of the remains has taken place. That's all there'll be until the afternoon. OK, lads,' said SuperQuigley, as he hung

up on the Garda Press Office. Let them deal with the queries now, he thought, instead of having the the local papers and local radio ringing him and putting him under pressure.

Morley had a sore head too. He lay back on the bed and cursed Manchester United. He hated United. He wished Roy Keane would get some terrible injury that would allow him to play in Ireland games only and that Beckham would get dandruff so bad, he'd be embarrassed to go out. He hated going to the pub and hearing all these fuckin' United fans who had been supporting their team for what, nearly three or four years now. Oh, yes, the genuine fans, the ones who can even remember Cantona.
Today he was in even fouler mood. United had just beaten Arsenal at Highbury and Vieira had stuck a head in Jaap Stam's face. But instead of taking the Dutchman's head off, Vieira had baulked. The two heads just locked together like horny cows rubbing against each other in a field. So when the phone rang, he realised later he had been very gruff when he answered it.
It was Fogarty, the man who thought he was Rock Hudson. Garda Rock Hudson.
'David.'
'Yeah.'
'I have something for ya. They're just after finding the body of a young wan out in Aran and we're fairly sure it's the Nolan kid from Newcastle. She had a row with her friends and then jumped in the river, or at least that's what it seems like. But we're not too sure. The boss here is going spare about it. That's seven suicides in the water since the beginning of summer. The fuckin' swans are complaining that the river's getting too crowded.'
Morley chuckled.
'Not in the Super's plan, at all. A clean summer, he said. He said he didn't want any bodies, a road accident or a murder or a suicide. No bodies and now they're popping up like flies. The city has gone mad. Now, I'm not saying it's drugs, but it could be. If ya get my drift. Or some shape of a cult. Now I'm not saying anything, but go and see what you can make of it.'
And then he was gone. Just like he fucked off out of Bar Cuba without paying for the drinks.

Morley dashed in and had a cold shower. It's easier to write when you feel clean and cool. You feel more confident on the phone as well.

He wasn't getting any sense out of the woman at the Suicide Help Line. He knew she'd been wary of him as soon as he got through. He knew she knew the tone of the article. She could see it already: *Suicide Crisis in City. Tribal Teens Going Crazy In Summer Sun.*

'I'm sorry I cannot talk about specifics. I can only talk about general statistics.'

'I know, but in the light of these deaths in Galway this summer, have you noticed an increase in any sort of problem?'

All he wanted was one decent quote. He needn't even name her. He'd put her down as a spokesperson, just so that there'd be one good quote, but she wasn't biting.

'Mr. Morley, we do not divulge such details to members of the media or to anyone at all and I suggest now that you get off the line in case genuine people are trying to get through.'

'Oh, genuine, as opposed to journalists, you mean?'

She didn't reply.

She'd seen it before when she worked in the Dublin office and had been told to refer all major media queries to head office. The only thing she was allowed to talk about was their annual report, so he'd have to twist the questions around to that.

'Listen, can we start again? Comparing your annual report which shows 25 suicides in Galway last year, are you alarmed that seven people have thrown themselves into the Corrib this summer so far?'

'Thrown themselves in. What a way to put it.'

'Well, taken their own lives then.'

'Do you know that?'

'Do I know what?'

'Do you know for sure they've taken their own lives?'

'Yeah, well, the Guards said, well, not for sure, but...'

'I can only comment on official Samaritans information. Not contribute to media speculation.'

'OK.'

'Right so. Now if you don't mind ...'

'Just one thing. These deaths. Are you concerned by them?'

'Deaths happen all the time. And of course we are concerned by them, but there may not be any link to one particular problem in the city. Where are you going with this? There is no connection.'

'But are you concerned?'
He wanted to ask her if she thought she was doing her fucking job properly. Maybe she was giving bad advice. Maybe when they rang up, she was being a wagon like she was now. He also wanted to ask her if she could hurry up and answer his question so that some poor bastard who wanted to get through on the line for help could do so. He held the phone away from his ear and waited for the rant to come to an end. "You want me to sensationalise this. You want me to say that we're panicking because so many suicides have been recorded in the west in the past. That we are concerned about this crisis and that we do not know what is responsible for the jump in people taking their own lives. But you and your sort don't seem interested in the causes of these figures, the heartbreak behind each story, the real tragedy that is suicide...'
That would do.
Fuck her.
He didn't need her anyway. She wouldn't be half as reluctant in the wintertime when they were looking for publicity for their sponsored walks or quizzes. It's a long road that has no turn.

Within 30 minutes, the tabloids were on to Morley about the find.
The tabloids heard it from the Garda Press Office and the duty editor rang Morley. It was always a bit embarrassing to get told by a Dublin hack that a major story was happening on your patch. It implied that you were sitting here in the west scratching your hole, so you had to let on that you knew about it, that you were working on it and that you'd e-mail the copy inside half an hour.
'We gave it to you, so do it for us and us alone,' said the Dub. Morley agreed, but he knew in his heart and soul that all the papers would take it. Exclusivity of details is one thing, but exclusivity for them all means more money and more sterling cheques.

The remains had been brought to University College Hospital before the Super had someone ring Paddy Nolan. They were flown in on the Sikorsky chopper, the big red and white one with the cute black nose. They had taken the body from the lifeboat station on Aran. Peadar Beag O Fatharta was at this stage drinking brandy in the American Bar and telling of his great discovery. This was even better than the ride with the Dutch bird.

Nightmusic

Patrice had been in the water for over a week now and even though the body was severely decomposed and ravaged by the creatures of the sea, there was little doubt that the the flap that was left of her face was that of the girl in the photo Paddy Nolan had given the Gardai. By now her picture had been put on posters around Shop Street, Quay Street and the nightclubs and in Corrib Village and in other places where people who might have seen her would congregate. SuperQuigley told the officers on the beat that they could start taking the posters down that evening, discreetly, after the family had been informed and the formal ID had taken place.

The phone rang.
'Super, it's David Morley here from the *Chronicle*.'
'Yes, David. I'm extremely busy now. Can I call...'
Morley knew he never called back.
'It's about the body, Super. Can you confirm that it's the body of the missing Galway teenager, Patrice Nolan?'
'David, contact the Garda Press Office and they will give you the latest information.'
'They don't have much to go on yet. I tried them.'
'Well, that's all we can release at the moment.'
'Super, I just need to have something to give the nationals. They won't want a name tonight. It'll do tomorrow, but can you give me something that the Press Office haven't been given.'
'That's the official position at the moment,' he said as he hung up.
Fuck him too.
Garda Kevin Loftus told him what he wanted to know. He played soccer with Morley, drank in the Imperial in the Square and over two pints, he told Morley what he wanted to know. Off the record, of course. That the body was that of Patrice Nolan, that her face had been eaten away and that she was fully clothed and more likely than not, she'd jumped into the water.
'If ya ask me, I think the father was riding her. But don't quote me on that.'
Morley didn't.
The line "It is believed that Ms. Nolan's father was riding her" was unlikely to appear in the story, but Morley took it down anyway, just to please Loftus who said he'd love another pint.

Nightmusic

It was First Friday in St Martin's. The usual auld ones were here for confession, rhyming off the harmless events that might have ranked for sins in 1920, but not in 2000, no matter how bad they were.
Malachy sat slumped in the seat when Nora Kennedy sat in opposite, but she'd seen him.
'How's your mother? Tell her I haven't seen her at the Bingo in the Silver Dollar for a while now.'
He wanted to say, 'Ya stupid cow, my mother is crippled she hasn't played fuckin' bingo for three years,' but he was in a church, a house of God, so he just smiled and said 'Any day now, she'll be with ye again.'
'That's good. Tell her I was asking for her.'
All fuckin' mad, they are, these auld ones. They must come in here to confess their madness and to seek a cure for it, but they weren't being given one obviously. Anyway, what's she asking about Mother for? He was glad he ran her when she came calling to the door last year. Even if she did help deliver him, but fuck, he didn't ask her. Nosey bitch just had to be there. Probably was in the GPO as well during the Rising. Has she heard something? Did she hear about Mother falling over the cat? Twice. Was mother talking to people about it and telling them that she didn't see the cat? Maybe it was time for her to fall over the cat again.

He always liked Fr. Ciaran. He was one of those young trendy priests who had introduced rock music into the church. He understood men a bit better than the others. He never went out of his way to embarrass ya in confession. And he knew his fishing. He'd come from a family who lived near Lough Corrib, so he could talk about dapping and trolling and Green Peters and mayflies and outboard motors until the cows come home. The door of the confessional opened and instead of going in, he put his head further into his hand. He wasn't going to go in and have Nora Kennedy listening to his sins from the other side, so he motioned that she could go before him. Today, he'd have the fun. She smiled suspiciously but accepted his offer and headed in. Two minutes later the other door opened, he went in, shut it behind him and pressed his ear to the wire to hear Nora Kennedy tell Fr. Ciaran how she had told a lie, and how she had cheated at 25 and how she had spread a rumour and so on so on. He took his head back from the cage. Nothing there to toss off to later.
He heard her mumbled act of contrition and then it was his chance.
'Bless me Father for I have sinned, it's been four weeks since my last

confession.'
Fourteen confessions a year, monthly and then one extra at Christmas and Easter when Mother came along.
'I used the Lord's name in vain, Father.'
'Yes.'
'I told lies, Father.'
'Yes.'
'And I was selfish, Father.'
That was the one. The selfish one. The humdinger.
Some priest had told them years beforehand that if they didn't want to mention wire pulling in confession then they could say they were selfish instead. Now the priest didn't exactly say wire pulling, he used some other term for it, but everyone knew what he was on about. He said that it covered a whole multitude of sins and that this would suffice instead of going into precise details and having the priest's hands wandering in the dark. But on reflection, you could say that selfishness can cover the likes of killing someone and even listening to Nora Kennedy's confession and looking through the windows of the holiday home off the Prom, where the group of girls were staying and where he could not see them undressing properly holding the binoculars with one hand and doing the bould thing with the other 'cos the lenses kept shaking. Yes, even that. Selfishness covered the lot.
But it wasn't Fr. Ciaran today. This priest was a tough bastard.
'What form did this selfishness take, my son?'
Stumped. And I'm not his son anyway.
'Well, I was sort of greedy and doing things to please myself.'
Did that sound too much like wire pulling? No.
The priest was silent for a minute and then decided to let it go as he rhymed into his long prayer. Malachy loved saying the Act of Contrition.
'Oh my God I am very sorry for all my sins because I have offended you...'
With those words he felt like he was back on the water again with the salt getting into the cuts on his hand cleansing out all the dirt in here and making them better for another day's work. Now technically, he was clean, and could go straight to heaven if he was struck down on the way home. The Lord loved him again. He was God's disciple and he was safe if anything happened to him on the way home.
But if he lived until tomorrow, there was bound to be some sort of

Nightmusic

temptation there again to make him do the things he did.

Nora Kennedy was still outside when he got out, doing the stations and genuflecting at each one. Surely she couldn't have been given that much penance for cheating at 25, when he'd just gotten away with murder and the other, ya know.

'The wages of sin, Watson, the wages of sin.'

* * * *

Nightmusic

Nora Kennedy took her time after leaving the church. She shuffled over to the petrol station across the road, picked up an *Advertiser* even though she'd get one through her door at home. She waited until he had come out of the church so she could get a better look at him. He came out a few minutes later, walking along with his hands in his pockets, got into his van and headed off in the direction of the city.
She had never trusted him. and she was going to tell them all at bingo about it. Too long spent at home with your mother is a bad thing. It softens the brain and the other areas too. You're no good to a woman after years of mollycoddling and living with your mother. That's why she had run all her lads. They had all grown up and left. Three of them had big houses in Knocknacarra and two others were working in Dublin. One in that Craig Gardiner place and the other in a company that makes boxes for computers out in Blanchardstown. But they were happy and had lovely girls. Unlike Malachy Lee, who did not seem to have any interest in girls at all, but who she thought was just slowly going a bit mad. And he had been such a nice lad, when he served mass over thirty years ago. Always spick and span and on time, unlike her fellas. But he was a bit of a loner now. She remembered how she'd thought he'd die the night he was born, but how he surprised them all. He was as bright as a button, reading and writing and well able to talk to tourists or the Guards. He helps them sometimes if there's a dog stuck in the river or something like that or someone trapped on Hare Island, but he had gone down a lot since she saw him last. He'd put on a bit of weight and now he had white sideburns which made him look older than 44. And he smelt a bit too. Nora had great time for him until the day he ran her from the house, and she hadn't gone back since. She knew that day that Delia was inside but he had that look in his eyes which made you not want to cross him, so she didn't.
When she got to Biddy Kerrigan's, she told her all about it.
'He's a bit weird. He's a bit not right in the head and it's all Delia's fault. She should have ran him years ago. Then he'd have some decent job instead of farting around with periwinkles and fishing and writing the odd letter to the *Advertiser* about the docks in the old days and all that.'
'Sure, that's the existence of a dreamer. Isn't the town full of them?' said Biddy.
She hadn't seen him for a while now. He used to go to the library in town a lot and carry home a whole bundle of books. She'd heard that

he joined up two or three times in different names years ago when they weren't as strict on those things and that he'd take home five or six books a week to read. 'Sure that's not right, either,' she said to her friends at the bingo session in the Dollar that night. They all nodded, but they wanted her to keep quiet, because Nora Kennedy's idea of whispering was a husky chatter and everyone in the hall knew Malachy Lee and it wouldn't be right to be talking about him like that.

There was a bigger than normal crowd at the bingo tonight, country buffers having come to town for it and that pissed off Nora no end. She used to like it when the bingo sessions were for the city folks and the country people had their own bingos in mangy halls. But now most of their bingos had shut and they were getting buses to town from as far afield as Mayo and Clifden and even up from Clare. Sure there was no chance of winning the jackpot at all in the Silver Dollar anymore or in the Seapoint for that matter. Too many tourists and bloody blow-ins.

'I said too many tourists here tonight,' she spat across the table

'Nora, shut up, I can't hear the numbers,' said Jack Hastings, who was playing three books and whose hands moved across the numbers like the pen on a lie detector.

'You're always bloody mouthing about something. If it's not the crowd here, it's Malachy Lee. Leave him alone, sure isn't he happy? If he wasn't going to confession, you'd be talking as well, or if he was off drunk every night of the week and falling down and cursing in the street like his father, and some of your lads,' he said to her.

That shut her up. For a second.

'Ya should have seen the way he was looking at me in the church. He goes to confession too often, as well. It's not right for a man. It's not safe for wimmen if these fellas start going to confession too much. Why can't he just go the normal amount, like twice a year. That's enough for a man.

Mark my words, that fella is a waster. It's not natural, I'm just saying it's not natural.'

She was down to one number for the house.

24.

That held her attention.

'Two and seven, twenty-seven.'

She had the sweats.

But she wasn't going to let on. When it came up, she'd politely say, 'House.'

'Two fat ladies, eighty eight.'
The hairs rose on the back of her neck.
She cleared her throat and straightened her scarf.
'Three and seven, thirty-seven.'
'Check,' said the countrywoman two tables down
'Fuck', said Nora, already starting into her quota for next week's confession.

* * * *

Nightmusic

The nationals loved Race Week. They liked nothing better than to have two or three pages of photos of babes and punters pictured "enjoying themselves at Ballybrit last evening." Morley liked it too because every national paper wanted to hear the lowdown on who was there and who was coming there. Of course, they all sent down their own reporters for a day or two and Morley would drink with them and mess with their heads a bit by telling them that this film star is coming and that film star is coming until they'd have their own reports so full of made-up shit, that by the Wednesday, the newsdesks would be ringing Morley to cover the Races for the rest of the week for them because they couldn't rely on their own eejits.

But now the Races were getting longer. Once they were just a few days long and now they were heading into a second week which meant that the amount of quality stories would be diluted to the point of non existence. The first few days were great because you could fill the reports with interesting stats and the old chestnuts about call girls coming west, the fat cats in the Fianna Fail tent, the rich winners, the all-night parties in the city hotels and the beautiful ladies contest on the Thursday which Morley noticed was becoming more of a sham as the years went by with professional models taking part. But he didn't care and he bet on every race secure in the knowledge that his losses would be well covered by his earnings from the week.

Morley liked the Races for other reasons as well as they signified the beginning of the end of the season in Galway. After this, the hordes of tourists would be heading back, the streets would get quieter, the traffic would actually move on the dozens of roundabouts around the city and Galway would gradually get back to normality.

Fogarty was looking forward to the end of Race week as well. With all Garda leave cancelled in Galway for the week, he had his holidays planned for the following ten days when Mary and the kids and himself would head up to Enniscrone and Donegal for a few days to a holiday home owned by a friend of his from back home.

For Race Week he had an annoying little trainee prick with him, just out of Templemore with a light blue strap on each shoulder signifying that he was just a learner guard, a 'yellapack' as some of the lads in the station called them.

He was from Tallaght and he reminded Fogarty of the young gurriers he used to chase around Neilstown when the place was bad a good few

Nightmusic

years back. When he spoke he sounded just like them and Fogarty wondered if one of those gurriers could now be a member of the force. But this fella was non-stop talking, asking stupid fuckin' questions all the time. What would ya do if this happened and what would ya do if that happened? Did ya ever get shot at? Who was the most famous one he'd ever arrested and why? Did he get to see many dead bodies? Was he ever on *Garda Patrol*? 'Garda fuckin' Patrol. How old did he think I was?' He could have filled him up with shit but he couldn't be bothered after a while, so he just played it cool. What he did hear the little prick saying though during the week was that he didn't want to end up in his late forties and still be just an ordinary guard. That bugged Fogarty and after that he didn't bother talking to the young fella at all and he sent him out to the racecourse gate on the Tuam road to direct traffic.

He collected a lunch voucher and headed along to the carvery for a bit of scran, being stopped occasionally along the way to tell people where the gates were, where lost children could be picked up and to wave at a few people like the Mayor and his wife, and Malachy Lee who helped them on the river from time to time.

People never realised just how sensitive the backs of your hands are or your elbows, but Malachy knew. He reckoned he had the most sensitive elbows and arms in Galway and he used them, especially during the Races to feel up any woman he wanted. Without them knowing, of course.
He reckoned his arms had some sort of sensor in them that could rub against a breast while walking through a crowd or the back of the hand would rub against the buttocks of a woman. They could almost draw a picture for him in his mind. The curve and the firmness of each would be transferred to his brain instantly, as if his hand was some sort of camera, converting an area into an image through the medium of touch.
When you're walking in a crowd and people are pushing behind you, they don't know what part of them is touching you and as long as it's not that phallic, most women don't bother to look. Pushing through crowds on Quay Street or at the racecourse, he reckoned he could feel the arses and tits of any woman he wanted, without having to resort to outright groping with hands. He set himself a challenge at Ballybrit on the Thursday to rub up the Best Dressed Ladies and the judges, and he

Nightmusic

succeeded, pushing behind them as they made their way through the crowds at Ballybrit.

With a race card in one hand and a pair of binoculars in the other, he looked very respectable. He even won money on a horse one day, but he didn't care about that. His race was far more exciting than any Galway Plate. And the going was far from soft. He loved it down around the parade ring area, because here everyone rubbed against each other. Big fat farmers and firm young women, gurriers in jackets and ties for the day. The announcer said one day that pickpockets were operating in the course, but fuck the pickpockets, this was far better. Maybe the announcer should have warned the women on the course that they were getting their arses felt up in between races, but he didn't, did he? That must mean I'm good at it, thought Malachy, as he made his way around the back of the new stand and headed off on another journey.

The Races were great because the women wore all kinds of light fabrics, cottons, lycras, linens. Linens aren't great because they give a distorted feeling, cottons are very smooth, but lycras are the best, as you can actually feel the wobbly buttock flesh through them. He reckoned he could tell if a woman was wearing a thong or silk lingerie or just the plain old cotton ones by just one rub of the back of his hand inadvertently across the bottom.

And he'd never been caught. There was just the once when his hand caught in a belt of an outfit one woman was wearing, but she laughed it off, thinking it had innocently gotten lodged there as he walked by. He was red faced and apologetic. She was great about it, very understanding, but they wouldn't all be like that.

Quay Street in summertime was also very good. He'd shave, and wear his good shirt and trousers and get his hair cut the weeks he did Quay Street. Then he could move through the crowds pushing this way and that, his hands rubbing against the bodies of the women as he sidestepped through the men on the narrow streets clogged with eager drinkers. He said 'sorry' and 'excuse me' a lot to cover himself but the effect was the same. It beat going to any disco. He reckoned he was getting more feels from a greater variety of women than any of the handsome fuckers who were there with their open-necked shirts, their Hugo Boss scents, their tanned chests, their ample heads of hair and their great teeth, talking shite to the girls all night. Why pay £8 for a club ticket when you can have all the gropes you want, without the responsibility? And yes, fuck it, he still respected himself in the morning.

Of course, it did not match the feeling he had when he got them back to the basement in the shed, but here the women were in their element. They were laughing and smiling and being sexy and flamboyant.

In the shed, they were different. They were frightened and peeing themselves and crying and moaning and breathing so hard their ribcages almost burst. So at least it was a chance to get to meet real women.

Night time in the city was a prime fishing area. Here there were loads of women in various levels of sobriety. The Judge had said there were dreadful women in Galway and that thought excited him, because he knew them, he could see them on the streets, drunk and shouting and giving off and having the craic. And asking for it. He was never tempted to do a pick off the streets of the city like this because it was too dodgy. Too much happens in the city centre. It is too alive, a beast in itself.

There was one night when he was looking at the photos from a Debs Ball in the windows of the *Connacht Tribune* office on Market Street that he thought there was a great chance, when a girl fell across the road after walking into a telegraph pole. She was drunk and her coins went all over the road. And her skirt went up her thighs and she was laughing. He looked up and down the road, not believing his luck, but it was too risky. The nightclub was just around the corner and there were always cars coming up Market Street or people walking up Church Lane, so he let it go. But it bothered him. It bothered him so much when he got home that he didn't go in. He looked up at the light upstairs and saw that Mother had made her own way up the stairs to bed. Then he turned the van and just drove straight out the Coast Road and took the turn up through the bog to the shed. There he lifted the door to the basement and took out the green box with the Polaroid photos, all arranged in envelopes. One for each girl, each taken from the neck down, each showing the white flesh of a photo taken in darkness with too much flash. He looked through these, wanked off to a selection of them and then drove home.

But it didn't compensate for missing the real thing.
Nothing compensated for the real thing.

Nightmusic

Paddy Nolan was becoming a sort of tragic celebrity. The day after the funeral he was back on Galway Bay fm. He wanted to thank everyone who had helped in the search for Patrice — the Gardai, the firemen, the neighbours and all her friends, yes even her friends. But the gratitude took up only three minutes and Keith Finnegan had him scheduled in for fifteen so talk soon came around to what exactly happened. A sobbing Paddy told the listeners that his daughter had given no indication that she was depressed or that she was in any form of trouble. She hadn't left a note so there were no immediate answers.
'There was nothing strange about her, Keith, like. She was just an ordinary happy girl who had her part-time job in the video store down the road. She liked to have fun and go to discos and that kind of thing. I cannot believe that she did what she did and we don't have any answers to them questions in our heads, like. It's very hard for us at the moment and we are praying a bit but there's still a pain in our stomachs when we wake up in the morning. Nawthing will make that go away, Keith. Ya can never tell about your kids when they go and do something like that.'

Paddy didn't say anything on the air but he knew that people were beginning to look at him a bit funnily. Daughters shouldn't be killing themselves for no reason, he thought they reckoned.
They were asking if she was pregnant and that if she was, who was the father of the baby and if she had been drinking and had been raped. The postmortem had shown she was not pregnant but there was no way of getting this across to the nosey fuckers who were spreading rumours. They all read the papers now and were able to read between the lines. The more grieving poor Paddy did, the more suspiciously they looked at him and wondered if he was slipping his daughter a length and asked was this what made her throw herself in the river. Or maybe he even threw her in himself.

He welcomed all the people who had come to the house and who had taken part in the search and who had shaken his hand firmly beside her coffin down in the funeral parlour in Munster Avenue, but now he found himself asking the questions. Every hand that grabbed his, he looked in their eyes and saw them questioning him and now he thought he could see the look in his wife's eyes, even though she couldn't possibly think anything, but maybe like the Gardai, she was keeping her options open. But now he couldn't handle it any more. He wished he was playing for Hibs again when he was strong and nobody fucked with him. Then he was fit and lean and strong, but now he looked in the mirror every morning and saw red eyes and greying hair and a face that said 'Why did she do it, Paddy? Ya might have been the hardest full back in the Galway and District League, but ya let yer family down. Ya didn't watch yer house, Paddy.'

What Paddy did know too was that there was a boyfriend out there somewhere who knew more about why she did it, but nobody would tell him who that was. Her friends were still saying nothing and the Guards weren't giving him much information either. And to top it all, he wondered if he ever did find out why she did it, what fuckin' good would it do? It wouldn't bring her back.

In Eglinton Street the postman was shitting a brick. He'd had a hard enough time trying to convince Sheila that there was nothing up when the Gardai called around a few weeks back and now he was sure there'd be more questions. Then Patrice was just a little ride from Newcastle.

Now she was a dead ride and dead rides don't get buried that easily.

He thought about going down to Mill Street and asking to see Garda Fogarty and telling him, well, telling him what he had told him already. There wasn't much he knew about her. That he only did it because it was handy. It was on a fuckin' plate, Garda, wouldn't you? But he knew that wouldn't go down well with Fogarty who would have no problem in giving his name to Paddy Nolan, and Nolan had more brothers than a family of knackers. Christ, he swore to fuck he'd never touch another young wan again and that he'd honour, obey and love his wife, but he'd promised to do that before and it hadn't done much good.

He shoved the mail into the bag, bolted it onto the bicycle and started out on his day's run, a worried postman.

* * * *

Nightmusic

Did you hear the one about Martin Kilkelly?
Everyone in Galway knew Martin Kilkelly.
Everyone who ever passed through Eyre Square did, anyway.
It was said that he'd accosted nearly everyone who stopped to look at the statue of Padraic O Conaire. Just like all the myths surrounding the winos in the Square, it was said that he was a fine footballer in his day and that he was a graduate of UCG, yes UCG, and that he had taken the wrong path,
and was a medical student who just couldn't summon the nerve to do his final exams.
And had hit the bottle and ended up on the Square. Others said that he was the inspiration to Mary Coughlan for her song about *Delaney's Gone Back On the Wine*, but sure wasn't it Delaney who inspired that. No, this was Martin Kilkelly and he was well known.
What wasn't said that often, though, was that he was a bloody nuisance and that he had seen the insides of the cells in the former barracks in Eglinton Street and the ones in Mill Street more often than the cleaners. They said he was getting too old to be on the streets and although he'd head off for a spell in some home for the alcoholic bewildered or some other clinic, he couldn't settle in a bed, preferring the hardness of the bench, the cold breeze that blew up around the Square and the camaraderie of the Bohermore lads who shared his drink and theirs.
Not being a regular shaver, when he'd return from the clinic, he always looked smaller, his hair cropped tightly and his face would be a myriad of little cuts where his beard used to be. However, the soap and water would not have washed away the leathery look of a face worn bare by the harshness of life on the streets. Martin liked being drunk and even when he was sober, he'd feign intoxication, just to scare the shite out of the tourists and the nuns, especially nuns. And there were always plenty of nuns in the Square, being so close to the bus and train station. Nuns are always on the move and being of a certain age, they loved to come and see the O Conaire statue.
He loved bothering nuns because they'd get embarrassed talking to him and scurry off. He loved bumping into them and getting a feel of their arses and asking them for money. It always worked, except for the time the missionary nun turned around and gave him a sort of liturgical bollocking in the middle of the Square. The lads were laughing their holes off back at the bench at the sight of the nun having Martin by the collar and pushing him up against the side of the statue.

Nightmusic

Good ol' Padraic O Conaire, their only mate in the Square, the only one who never gave them any guff. Martin sat by the statue for the guts of twenty years and told tourists that this man's most famous book was about his dirty black ass. In all his time there, he hadn't met anyone who had read the O Conaire stories, but nevertheless, they'd come and sit anyway and take pictures of the funny little stone man.

Mother knew Martin. She knew him from the old days and had plenty of stories about him. He used to come to the house and do some odd jobs after Father died. Mother would tell Malachy to help Martin in the shed with the turf and so he often did, pushing a wheelbarrow up a plank which led up the stack of turf and then tipping it all in at the back of the shed. It was important to get it all in before dark because the Shantalla lads would be up and they'd be pocketing it. There was always a few bottles of stout in it for him, plus his dinner and a few bob. But the pile of turf grew like a mountain at the front half of the shed and there was a valley at the back, where they'd doss and eat sweets and smoke fags even though Mother would kill Martin for showing her young son the ways of the world, but she needn't have worried too much.
... it was here Martin told Malachy how to say fuck and bollocks and told him what tits were.
... it was here he told him about a ride he got off some big black woman in England.
... it was here he showed him how to drink a bottle of stout without stopping for air.
... and it was here one day he forced Malachy up against the turf, pulled down his short trousers and entered him from behind forcing his face into the peat with every thrust for the two minutes it took for him to let go of the back of Malachy's neck and offer him another swig of the bottle and tell him not to mind the pain in his arse because it'd go after a while and not to tell anyone.
Kilkelly was no UCG graduate, failed doctor or fine footballer. He was a bum all his life and he seemed the ideal choice for the first one. Sure who'd miss him?

Still, though, it's amazing how hard it is to kill someone. No, not making the decision to kill them, but battering the fuckin' life out of them. Kilkelly's head had taken four wallops of the hurl and he was still moaning. There was no point moaning here in the cellar of the shed, because there wasn't a house for miles. You'd think someone who lived a life like he did would just give up and die. What had he to live for but cold nights in the Square and even though he was drunk, he suddenly regained a sense of sobriety as each slap of the ash hurl cracked into his head. But no, he had to do it the hard way, staggering about and moaning and reaching out for something to grab. But there was nothing there so he fell again and two more cracks hit his skull. This time, it was a different sound. Malachy used the edge of the hurl instead of the flat bit which merely gave you a hard slap. This time, there was no crack, just a sort of mushy slap and funnily enough, that's the one that must have finally put him away. After that he didn't get up. His legs quivered a bit and even that stopped after a few minutes.

And that's how he did his first one. The one they say is the hardest. He dropped him with a rock tied to his legs somewhere off Spiddal, well out and he sank like the proverbial thing that was tied to his leg. He thought about it a lot those first few days. He had often wondered what it would be like and now he knew he could do it, he felt he had crossed some sort of threshold. Now it was limitless. You see, the only thing that stops us all from killing each other is our inability to live with the thought of what we have done. If we could do the fuckin' thing, absorb it in our minds and get on with our lives, there's no telling what sort of beasts we'd become. And maybe that would settle a lot of arguments. Sure killing was alright until we got a fuckin' conscience about it.

And after a few days, he was comfortable with it. It was ideal. The bastard deserved it for ridin' him in the turf, he thought. And sure who would miss him? Even those who are supposed to be looking after his likes would give up after a few days in the thinking that he had snuck onto a freight train and made his way to Dublin like he did before. The guards were asked to keep an eye out for him, but he never showed up again. That was in 1989 and nobody ever mentioned him again, apart from Mother who said that you'd miss him for bringing in the turf even though they didn't have turf in the house for fifteen years. Anyway, she had a son now who could bring in
the turf on his own. He'd look after her and make sure she didn't fall over the cat anymore.

Now that's the one about Martin Kilkelly.

* * * *

Nightmusic

The release of the Leaving Cert. results is a great earner for the reporters in the regions. You see, most of the Dublin papers wouldn't bother their arses getting results reaction from Dublin schools, because let's be honest, there's fuck all to get overjoyed about there, is there?

No, they wanted brainy, wholesome, healthy looking kids from the country, with strong jaws and long hair and unpronounceable fucking names in Irish. The nationals were so afraid of thinking local, they went out of their way to ignore Dublin schools.

So that's where Morley came in. They'd ring him up the day before the results, tell him to go down to the schools in Galway, meet a few of the students, get their reaction and their photographs and then lob it all into the newsdesks via the e-mail.

Ja Duggan was the photographer who was always keen to make a few bob on the side and with Morley getting all the best stories, the two worked as a team, unknown to the papers in Dublin.

And to make it easier, they'd had the students picked a week beforehand — good looking birds and football-playing fellas, all of whom were confident of getting good results and who wouldn't mind posing for the papers. Ja would get the pictures, give Morley the names and so when the editors put the text and pictures together at the newsdesks, they were thrilled to see that there were pictures of some of those quoted. Coincidence. Conspiracy more like.

Ja would get their pictures early in the morning and Morley would have the story written and on the newsdesks in Dublin, Cork and Belfast as soon as the news editors clocked on at 11.

There was one year he fucked up the results story in the *Chronicle* and had the quotes of the principals all mixed up, so the head of the fashionable boarding school was quoted as saying he'd be glad if half his class made it onto FAS courses, while the head of the run-down school was on record as saying that most of his class were going to University.

And schools get so crabbed when you say anything about them.

The principal of the fashionable school had come in to the Chief to complain. The head of the run-down school stayed away. He was thrilled.

'Does your reporter not realise the importance of educational reputation nowadays? Schools are no longer community projects, they are a large business and mistakes like this create the wrong impression. And that impression could result in parents deciding not to send their children to my school,' he told the Chief, but the Chief nodded and then told him to fuck off, that he had a paper to get out, that he'd print a clarification buried deep inside somewhere near the farm page and finished off by saying he never went to a fashionable school and look how he turned out.

Ja and Morley weren't the only ones who liked exam results time. As he'd leave mass on the feast of the Assumption, Malachy Lee always knew that later that night there'd be prime fishing. They'd be like shoals of little fish coming towards the nets. Sometimes blindly, not knowing where they were going. But ultimately facing the hands of the fisherman. Every August for years, he used to bring Mother to Knock on this day, but in recent years, the journey and the crowds were too much for her, so she stayed at home and said her prayers there. She said she didn't like it anymore anyway and that it was full of plastic statues and unscrupulous street hawkers. 'Bit like the temple when our Lord threw the head, Mother,' he said, only too keen to put her off the idea of travelling to the Mayo shrine when the city was full of young ones.
'So I won't bother with Mass today,' she'd say.
'God won't mind, Mother. He won't knock ya back at the gates of Heaven just because you couldn't make it to Mass a few times in the twilight of your life.'
And she'd say, 'Off you go, Malachy and say a prayer for sinners,' and that always made him think of her burning his books and telling him to forget Mozart and Sherlock Holmes and God knows what other sins she did over the years. However, if she couldn't make it to Mass, he'd have to go through the Rosary with her and not just five decades but another five as well for good measure. He'd kneel there with his arms into the cushion of the chair, facing the Sacred Heart lamp and hum the responses to her slow Our Fathers and never ending Hail Marys. When he was younger he used to time himself with a watch with a second hand that he got in Dillons and see how quickly he could make it through a decade, but then Mother had caught him and confiscated the watch. For ages. Just like the books, but he got the watch back. It hadn't been thrown into the range.

Hundreds of them would be gathered down around the Spanish Arch, sitting there on the edge of the river, yelping and yowling about their results, but no matter how pissed they were, would they ever fall in? Oh

Nightmusic

no, they needed some help for that. But if you drove around an hour or two later, they'd be even worse. Then they'd be more vulnerable as they'd have scattered all over the city and you'd find them on roads leading out to the suburbs, falling across in front of cars or leaning on poles puking up. He drove past Mill Street, where the lights were on all over the building in expectation of a busy night. Down Dominick Street and over onto Fr. Griffin Road and back into town again past Jury's. They were everywhere, like ants let loose after someone had kicked over their anthill, stumbling around, arms around one another singing and shouting and carrying bottles. He went around by the Docks and looked up at the lifeboat station. The lights were on there, too. They were on standby as well in case someone fell in, with their fucking high tech equipment and their radars and radios and echo sounders and big orange boat so that it could be seen from the sky and their helicopter backup and all that. Much more than I used to have when I was the riverman for the guards, he thought.

The best fish, they come out of the water just when you are not expecting them. They are the ones you don't have to play with too much as they sort of happen onto your hook and are in the boat before you or they know it.
This was an easy fish. Malachy couldn't believe his luck when he saw her, leaning against the pole at the end of the Prom. Right at the place where the walkers kick the wall on their halfway point of their summer prom walks. But there was no-one else to kick the wall now as it was well past 2 a.m. She'd obviously been sick and as he came closer, she came onto the road and raised an arm to hail him down.
He leaned over and opened the door.
'Are ya all right, luv?'
'How much to Knocknacarra? I have to get there.'
'Hop in, I'll get ya there.'
She smiled and sat in onto the seat, her high heels crumbling to one side under her as she tumbled into the van.
'Were ya celebratin?'
'Yeah, have to go to Knocknacarra.'
'Doing the Leaving, were ya?'
She didn't answer, but her stomach heaved as if she was about to get sick.
'Here, have another drink from this. It'll make it easier,' he said handing

Nightmusic

her the bottle of whiskey.
'I want vodka.'
'Take that first and I'll get ya vodka then.'
She said nothing, just sort of stared at him.
She had long brown hair and was wearing a dark denim jacket that hung loosely open over a pink top and a black skirt.
She took the bottle from him, smelt it and then took a short drink from it and then another.
'There, that make ya feel better?'
Again she said nothing but she dozed off just as he passed Barna Woods and didn't wake again until he had the van reversed into the shed and the lights off. He went and opened the doors to the basement and he carried her down, closing the doors behind him. She was light and her legs felt really smooth so he explored a bit, but then he remembered the insulating tape.
She awoke with a start when the tape went around her mouth the first time, but her arms and legs were tied too so she couldn't move. He had piled her clothes on the chair beside the table and had removed most of his too, before he took the first photos and let his hands explore further the smoothness of the body of a Leaving Cert.

He always blessed himself before he tossed off, sort of asking for some form of forgiveness in advance and remembering the words of Father Curtin who had told him about Onan from the Bible and the terrible sins he had committed while touching himself.
He never knew there was anything about that sort of stuff in the Bible, but then he discovered Genesis chapter 38:9 and had memorised the bit when Onan was told by Judah to 'go into your brother's wife and perform the duty of a brother-in-law to her and raise up offspring for your brother. But Onan knew the offspring would not be his, so when he went in to his brother's wife, he spilled the semen on the ground lest he should give offspring to his brother and what he did was displeasing to the Lord and he slew him.'
Father Curtin was always on about that piece when Malachy was an altar boy and was helping him count the collection on a Monday night in the priest's house. He'd get very angry that this warning was being ignored and he'd hold Malachy close and tell him this and shake him and shake himself until his anger sort of subsided. Malachy wanted to ask the priest questions about this Onan character whose fifteen

minutes of fame included refusing a ride in the Bible and then getting killed for tossing off instead, but Father Curtin never wanted to talk about that much afterwards because then he'd be sweating and shaking and different and just wanting to make sure that Malachy got home okay.

But if Father Curtin was trying to put Malachy off touching himself, he did a bad job of it, because the first thing Malachy did when he went to the library was find that chapter and read it, and the auld wans in the library would see him and say things like 'Isn't the child great for reading the Bible?' when unknown to them he was reading about the world's first wanker in the world's best selling book.

There was great stuff in there that a lot of people didn't know about at all. You had to read between the lines to find the juicy bits but there was killing and rape and adultery and buggery and sodomy and other things in there as well if you only took the time to find them. Which he had. He had listed the chapters in a notebook under the heading of The Best Bits of the Bible and had them ordered chronologically.

Things must be done decently, Watson, and in order.

He was a careful undresser as he knew that putting clothes back on someone can be difficult, so everything was on the right way around or they'd catch ya out. They'd know that something was wrong and then they'd be on to ya, but he was too cute for that and all items were laid on the chair in the exact order he'd taken them off, and the right way around. Black panties, the black bra, the pink top, the shoes, the skirt. When he was finished, he put them back on, loosening the tapes and then tying them again, but this girl was lapsing in and out of consciousness and was in no mood for a fight.

He knew that he could probably have let her away back near Salthill again, but she had seen him and there was no knowing really how drunk she was, so he knew there was not going to be any university for this one. No nights spent drinking in the fancy pubs around town, no going with her friends to Mozart concerts in the Aula Maxima. In a nutshell, none of the things he'd have liked to have had, but didn't because Mother was an ignoramus from the country who burned books. She wanted him to suck up to Uncle Peadar and get left some of the land. Now he had the bog and the ruined farmhouse and the shed with the cellar, and he was certainly making use of it in a way Mother would never understand.

Coming back into town, he cut across the Barna Road to Moycullen and down into Tonabrucky, cutting over Circular Road until he came to Bushy Park and Dangan. It was quiet here at this hour of the night, so he drove the car down the roadway, past the college sports grounds and over to the river. In the dark, Menlo Castle looked imposing and eerie, but it was all quiet. He had freewheeled the van down the last bit of the road, with the lights turned off, the only sound being the crunch of the gravel under the tyres. Just to make sure, he got out and sat there for ten minutes to see if there was any sound to be heard, but there was nothing apart from the far away yells of celebrating teenagers making their way across the Quincentennial Bridge, far upriver. Even though he was wearing his oilskin waterproofs, he had his waders on, the long green ones that Mother had bought for him in the fishing shop about ten years ago. They were folded down on the outside, so he pulled them up to waist level and went back to the van. She had gotten sick again and her eyelids just blinked a little, before she passed out once more.
Carrying her to the riverside, he took the tape off her legs and her mouth and waded out into the river holding her in his arms. Then getting himself soaked in the chilly water, he lowered her quickly so that the cold water would not bring her around. He held her down, about two feet under the surface. There were a few bubbles and some splashing as her legs began to kick slightly. Then he counted to 50, said a decade of the rosary, the slow way, and felt her whole body go limp before pushing her out into the river where the current was heading back towards the city and the last of her classmates who'd be wondering where she was gone to. Strangely he felt a bit morose after this one, so he pushed in the cassette into the player, turning up the volume just a little bit so that he could hear the soprano sing out the mournful airs of *Soave Sia Il Vento*, from the first act of *Cosi Fan Tutte*. He listened to this for three minutes, then sat up, started the van and headed back home to Mother.

* * * *

Nightmusic

SuperQuigley hadn't slept well that night. He had a dream that he got a call from the Commissioner in the Phoenix Park who told him he was a useless fucker and that the city was going to hell under him. So the first thing he did when he woke up was ring Mill Street and say that he'd be in at 12 for an inspection.

'A fuckin' inspection. He can inspect this,' said Garda Kevin O'Shea, grabbing his crotch as he rooted through his locker for a tie. 'It'd be more in his line to be getting the fifty extra heads we need here rather than a fuckin' inspection,' but then he remembered that the Inspector was behind the next line of lockers so he shut up.

They ran up and told the detectives in the crime room as well and they emptied old coffee cups and smelly sandwich wrappers into bins.

There hadn't been an inspection at the station for years. In fact, none of them could remember one out in Salthill or Tuam either. Why he was holding one now was beyond them. But they still had to get ready for it and drop whatever cases they were working on, so that they could look OK.

Four of them ran down to Dominick Street to the barbers for the quickest cut that the barber ever gave and two others took out the iron from the stolen goods store to give their shirts and trousers a good press. A can of Lynx was thrown from officer to officer in the locker, the air a sweet smell of honey and lavender and Egyptian Breeze.

They had been told about this in Templemore — that they had to have the hair the regulation length and that it should not be protruding out from under the caps, sideburns were a bit of a no-no and every officer was expected to have shaved before he reported for duty. Trousers and shirts had to be pressed, belts had to be straight, and caps had to be in good condition.

Only the female Gardai could relax. He was unlikely to pick on them. He was always careful before he said anything to them, stopping and thinking before picking his words carefully. Noreen Sheedy and Catherine Kelly sat back with their feet on the desk and cups of coffee in their hands and laughed and watched as the men ran around, but they eventually got up and took over in the Communications Room so that the lads on duty there could spruce up.

'Noreen, will ya take over for a few minutes 'til I get this sorted out?' said Garda Martin Hannon as he pointed to his hair and handed her the ear piece. It was an hour before normality was resumed at the station, but by then, twenty four of them had taken haircuts, and four others had swapped trousers with the lads clocking off.

The inspection was held in the large conference room on the third floor, the one where they all normally gathered for the TV cameras when there was s a murder investigation, the ones where they had to look serious, determined and mean for the cameras. Today, however, they felt a bit small. Grown men having to show that they were able to wash themselves.
'It's a fuckin' disgrace,' said Fogarty and of course, the Super heard him as he moved along the line. They watched as he shuffled around the room and of course, he stopped at Fogarty again and told him to shove his shirt into his trousers and to shine his shoes properly and to get himself a proper haircut. He picked on a few others as well and then told them all that standards had to be set and had to be maintained. Then he thanked them for their time and asked them all to go back to their duties. Which they did, grudgingly. With their new haircuts and the smell of Lynx off them.

* * * *

Paddy Nolan was surprised when Garda Fogarty came to the door. Even though he was in his civvies, Paddy recognised him from the funeral and how he'd said he'd get to the bottom of it.
'Come in, come in,' he said, beckoning the burly Garda through to the front room where a soccer match was on the telly. Fogarty didn't recognise any of the teams.
'Who's playing?'
'Alaves and Santander,' said Paddy, as he signalled for Fogarty to sit down on the couch.
'Who would they be when you'd be at home?'
'Spanish teams. They're big in Spain. Sky show all these foreign games and they're great if you're a soccer fan. They keep your mind off things for a while, so they do.'
'How have ya been keeping?'
'Oh, good days, bad days. Mostly bad days, though. Have ya found anything? Is that why you're here?'
'No, no news at all. My visit isn't strictly official.'
'Why? Is there something you're trying to find out?'
'Just trying to make sense of it all. It bugs me to see things like this have

no explanation. And there won't be much coming out of the inquest either.'
'No, I suppose not.'
'All that there will be are the technical details of Patrice's death. Not much in the way of reasons, I'm afraid, Paddy.'
'There was one thing I meant to ring ye about this week. About three weeks ago, we got a call from the travel agents in town to say that Patrice's tickets were ready. She was going to Paris for her 19th birthday and had booked them back in February with the two girls. Got a good price for them then,' he said as he tore open a pack of ten Carrolls and lit one and then threw the packet across to Fogarty, who shook his head.
'So she was going on a holiday, then? She had plans. That makes it all the more strange that she would do anything like that,' said Fogarty.
'It's strange, all right. I know she wouldn't do anything like that. It's fucked me up big time. I can't concentrate on anything. Every time I think about doing anything for the house or the job, I wonder what's the fuckin' point, ya know? Before, every time I did a job like that I'd be thinking of what we'd do with the shillings, like. Now, it doesn't matter because after breaking your hole workin' all your life, your daughter ends up dead in the water, d'ya know what I mean?' he said, wiping a tear from his eye.
Fogarty put his hand over and squeezed Paddy's shoulder.
'And how's your missus?'
'She's fuckin' worse. She's on some tablets that Dr. Maguire gave her, supposed to help her sleep, but they don't and they make her a fuckin' zombie during the day. Jaysus, Noel, you wouldn't know what a thing like this would do to ya. It's fucked us all up. We might as well all be in the river. Even the kids at school got stick about it. They came home here crying that their pals were saying their sister was a druggie and a dopehead and all that. But she wasn't. I could bring the drugs squad and the dogs into that room of hers and they'd die of fuckin' starvation. She's as clean as a whistle in that way. I know she drank. I found a Smirnoff bottle here and there, but that doesn't make ya jump in the river. D'ya know what I'm saying, like?'
'Yeah, I agree with ya. It seems strange. Between ourselves, there have been a few deaths like that this year that don't quite add up. Now the Super is worried about them too, but we don't have a clue where to start.'

Nightmusic

'I know, sure where do ya start in a thing like this? It's shockin', so it is.'
'I don't want to offend ya or anything, Paddy, but do ya think there might be some sort of a cult involved? Was she into any o' that stuff?'
'Cults, is it? No way. Our Patrice wasn't into anything that didn't have a designer label on it. She'd no time for that shit at all. She barely went to Mass.'
'Nothing has come up on her credit cards or anything since? No strange payments to anyone or anything?'
'No, we've looked at the lot, amn't I telling ya?'
Fogarty wondered whether to tell Paddy about the Postman but decided against it. He knew Paddy would go around and kill him and then where would ya be? If he was meant to know, he'd find out himself.

The Postman got a call in at work in Eglinton Street asking him to meet Fogarty. He seemed startled and started stammering on the phone.
'I can come down there and meet ya at the post office, but I think you'd prefer to see me in private. I'm in civvies anyway, so don't worry yourself. I'll be upstairs in News at Ten. Ya can't miss me. I'll be down the back with a pink carnation stuck up me hole.'
He was over in about ten minutes, looking sheepish and thin. Kind of starved looking, Fogarty watched him come in and wondered what a scrawny fucker like that was doing getting rides off good-looking young ones. Maybe it was easier to get the ride nowadays, he thought to himself. The ride was more the starting point rather than the grand finale nowadays.
Postman saw him and came down, sitting quickly into the chair.
'I've only ten minutes or so. I took my break early.'
'You'll be as long as this takes, so ya will. Now I'll have a cup of tea and one of them buns with the chocolate, and whatever you're having yourself,' said Fogarty, without handing over any cash.
Postie went up and bought the grub and returned with the full tray looking for all the world like Oliver Twist.
'Now I want you to tell me the dates you were with Patrice Nolan and give them to me nice and accurately and tell me where you were with her.'
Postie started rhyming off days and places, where he met her and how old she said she was and how she said she liked older men because the fellas she had were spotty.
'Now did she ever say anything to ya about being in a cult or anything?'

Nightmusic

'No, I don't know where you're going with this but...'
'Listen here, ya little shit. I'm on my way over to Newcastle now, so I could be going through this with your wife and asking her the same questions, so the answers better be pretty fuckin' lucid, d'ya know what that means, lucid?'
Postie nodded and answered the questions, telling Fogarty that Patrice never gave any sign of doing anything extreme like that. No, she never took any drugs. Her drink was Smirnoff Ice and she was on the pill. He'd been with her five or six times, mostly in his mother's house while she was in hospital.
Fogarty thought that was disgusting, bringing home a young one to your auld mother's bed and riding her there. He wanted to throw the pot of tea over the little squirt, but the place was packed.
He took a few notes here and there, an action which made Postie even more nervous as people were looking at him as if he was being interviewed by a reporter or something. He didn't drink his tea, but Fogarty scoffed down the chocolate bun and then took the Postie's.
Seemingly Patrice was besotted with this bloke and she told him everything about herself, but there was no sign that she was into any weird shit.
'She liked to go and get drunk but she wasn't keen on any drugs or anything. She was saving her money for a trip to France or something, so she was tight enough. In that department, I mean.'
Fogarty didn't like that remark. Postie was getting smarter as the questions went on. Still, he shouldn't have spoken that way about the dead.
'Can I go now?'
'Yeah. On yer way, but if ya try any stunt like that with anyone else, I'll be on to ya. D'ya hear?'
Postie nodded and smiled so that people would not think he was getting a serious warning, and left the table, looking around to see if anyone was watching him, and wondering what two grown men were whispering about at a table. He turned around the corner and went down the stairs and back down to Eglinton Street.

Fogarty hoped he'd have better luck with Patrice's friends, Shelley and Nicola. Both of them were working in boutiques in town in the new shopping centre and were dolled up to the nines when he called in to see them, but he decided to meet them after work in the flat they had

Nightmusic

in Newcastle. Whatever about meeting the Postman, he couldn't be seen meeting the two young wans in a bar as they'd immediately attract attention with their wild hair and perfect makeup which made them look more 35 than 18.
When he came into the flat they had the telly on and were watching Ally McBeal.
'D'ya watch this?' said Shelley.
'I've seen it. The wife likes it. I can't make head nor tail of that shite, with dancing babies and singing, and men and women pissing in the wan jacks, it's totally unrealistic.'
'No, it's great. It's young, ya see.'
'Well, I'll take your word for it,' he said.
'We told Mr. Nolan most of the stuff about Patrice, but we didn't tell him about the fella she had,' said Nicola. 'He'd have hit the roof. But d'ya think he was involved?'
'I don't know. You tell me,' said Fogarty taking a seat at the kitchen table.
'Will ya have a cup of coffee, Guard?'
'Aye, I will.'
'We'd forgotten about the holiday the time she, ya know, died. We were all going to Paris next month. We got a Ryanair flight and we were staying in a hotel over there. Just the three of us, our first holiday together.'
'Why Paris? I thought Ibiza would be more your style?'
'Twas cheap and we were never there. Patrice wanted to see where Lady Diana died.'
'Princess Diana,' said Nicola. 'Ya said Lady Diana.'
'Whatever,' said Shelley. 'Patrice was very upset when Di croaked in the crash. And we wanted to see Paris anyway.'
Fogarty wrote down the name of Princess Diana in his notebook. Jaysus, SuperQuigley will love this.
And maybe Mohammed Al Fayed.
'Listen girls, can ya rack your brains for me and tell me if there was any sign at all that Patrice would have killed herself. She didn't leave a note or anything, so it's a bit strange.'
'No guard, she never gave us any idea she was like that...'
'She was like a bitch on the last night we saw her, though, but that was just her. Typical.'
'Tell me about the row,' he said, as he continued writing into his

battered notebook.
'We were telling her to stop seeing the fella in the post office as he was only using her. We told her that she was being an eejit but she couldn't accept it at all and told us we were jealous,' said Nicola.
Shelley continued.
'She told us we were a shower of fuckers and we had this blazing row just down from the roundabout on Bishop O'Donnell road and she went home across the fields like.'
'Across the fields to her house. She only lives over there a bit. She always goes that way and that's the last we saw of her.'
'Did you see anyone strange there who might have followed her or anything?'
'No, the row was on the side of the street and she was roaring.'
'She was a bit drunk...'
'She was well on it.'
'There was the van, though. Remember, Nic, the green van that drove by and slowed down and then revved up again. That went by twice, but we thought it was only some knackers being nosey.'
'A green van. What type?' asked Fogarty draining the bottom of the coffee cup.
'Ya know, the knackers type van, that sort of one,' said Shelley.
A green Hiace van. Must be fuckin' hundreds of them in Galway, he thought.
But he wrote it down anyway.

* * * *

The kids were in bed when he got in, but Mary was still pottering around in the sitting room with her hand down behind the couch.
'I can never find that remote control.'
'Try under the cushions, luv.'
She reached into the corner of the couch and pulled it out, jabbing it in the direction of the telly, knocking down the sound.
'Where were ya?'
'I went to see that Paddy Nolan and a few others about his daughter...'
'Did the Super send ya? Is there any news?'
'Yeah, he sent me. It's a bit hush-hush like. There's no news, divil the bit, but I'm not convinced that she killed herself. There were no signs. There's always something if they killed themselves. Some sign. Some

nervous thing. A row or something like that or tablets, but she was on nothin' like that at all.'
'Was she pregnant?'
'No, she wasn't. She was havin' a fling, though, with a married bloke from Newcastle.'
'Really.'
'I spoke to him but he's not involved. Just a sleazeball. I could tell Paddy, her father. He'd kill him.'
'Sure, it'll do feck all good to her now, anyway. It won't bring her back.'
'No, but it might stop some other wan doing the same thing.'
'Are ya tired? Ya look like shite. Quigley is working ya too hard. The top brass would never do the dirty work. Bet he's at home with his feet up, a glass of wine in his hand, and watching telly with his wife like you should be.'
'I've never seen his wife.'
'Ha, fuckin, ha. I meant with me.'

He hated when she spoke like that, emphasising rank and in a subtle way underlining that he'd never made it. She was in a mood tonight. Her face had that lived in look that all guard's wives have. The one where her eyes have been stretched from nights waiting and wondering, her hair clipped back and her hand holding the umpteenth cigarette she'd had that day.
'I do it because I care, Mary, and maybe I'm a fuckin' eejit.'
'I rest my case, yer honour,' she said sarcastically.
She ignored him. and switched back on the telly. To that fuckin' French one, TV Five, or Teeveesanque as she called it. He hated that because he knew she was doing it to spite him. He hated it when she clammed up.
'I'm sorry, Mary. Listen I'll put on the kettle.'
'Don't bother. I'm going to bed soon anyway.'
He hated arguing like this. He wanted her to look at him and then he didn't want her to look at him, because no matter how much she loved him, it would be tested now by the state of him. He was tired, red-eyed, unshaven, smelly and he wanted a bath. She looked over at him and then back to the TV where Gerard Depardieu was screwing some young one. Fat fucker. That's what being able to speak French does for ya. Fuck, Depardieu was uglier than the postman. What was Fogarty doing wrong?

Nightmusic

Mary turned up the volume and he left the room, heading up the stairs, stopping off to lean into the hot press to feel the barrel and see if there was enough water for a bath. There wasn't, so he knocked on the switch, before making his way down the corridor to the end room. He opened the door silently. The Pokemon light was on at the far locker, throwing a sea of yellow illumination across the room and over the two faces of Caoimhe and Niamh. Both were asleep, each clutching a cuddly bear. He looked at them and thought about how innocent they were, here asleep in their beds with their minds away in some fluffy world of dreams — a world devoid of suicides and drugs and postmen riding young wans. They were nine and seven. Christ they were only about ten years younger than Patrice Nolan. In ten years time would they be experiencing the same traumas, he wondered? Would they be taken advantage of by married men who should know better and would they be flinging themselves into the river for some unknown reason? He felt a chill down his spine at the thought of it and he started to cry. Just a sob at first and then a heave of his shoulders which woke up Caoimhe and then Niamh.
'Hello, Daddy.'
'Go back to sleep.'
'Mammy made a trifle for us this evening. It was lovely. It was really creamy.'
'We left some in the fridge for you,' said Niamh. 'Do you want to eat it now?'
'No, not now, Daddy isn't hungry.'
'But Daddy, we kept it for you. Will you promise to eat it later?'
'I promise,' he said with another sob.'
'Are you crying, Daddy?' asked Caoimhe.
'Why are you crying?'
'I'm crying because I love you both to pieces,' he said, reaching out and grabbing the two of them who pulled themselves as close as they could to his chest as his arms enveloped them.
'Now, go back to bed and have plenty of nice dreams.'
'We will, Daddy. You won't forget the trifle.'
'I'll have it before I go to bed,' he said. 'Now, plenty of sweet dreams.'
Sweet dreams, a world removed from the reality of the city outside their windows.

As he sank into the lukewarm bath he looked down at his expanding stomach. He had tried to lose some weight last year but it was difficult. He lost four or five pounds but then he put it back on again, and more. He used to joke to Mary about fat fellas who couldn't see their willies when they stood up. Now that was happening to him and either way it was worrying as it meant either his belly was expanding or his willy was getting smaller. But lying here in the bath, things didn't look too bad as the flab fell to the bottom of the tub.

His mind went back through the meetings of the day. These are the people I'm supposed to protect, he thought, bringing to mind the Jack Nicholson speech from *A Few Good Men*. The "You can't handle the truth" one. Nicholson told Tom Cruise that when he was in bed at night, it was he and the other soldiers who stood on the wall to protect him. The people he had met today were the people he was being paid to protect. The people of the city — the worried father, the randy postman and the lonely friends. They were the ones he had to protect every night when he drove into Mill Street. But how do you protect these people from themselves? That was the problem.

He splashed the water up on his head and brushed back his hair, making him look like Elvis. And then he dried himself with a big pink towel. When he walked into the bedroom afterwards, shaven and clean, and with a bowl of fresh trifle in his hand, Mary was sitting up in bed with another cigarette and a book, but she smiled at him with his hair standing up, so he burst into a line of 'I ain't nothing but a hound dog...' and she laughed.'
'Ya know, ya look right like Elvis.'
'Well thank you, ma'am.'
'I mean how he looked at the very end.'
'Oh, is that right? Well, I'd better not go and have a shite then and that'd finish me off altogether.'
He finished the trifle, then he took her hand, knocked off the light and made love to her until they fell asleep in the spoons position an hour later.

* * * *

Nightmusic

The Super had the team out early two days later after Jessica Kelly's body was found at the Salmon Weir bridge just under the cathedral. One of the salmon anglers who was walking along the slipway spotted the bright colours of her top in the water and raised the alarm. She hadn't come home the previous day, but she still hadn't travelled that far, her journey broken by the bashing her body took against the steel gates and concrete pillars between Dangan and the Salmon Weir.
Everyone thought Jack Charlton or some other famous angler was fishing there again, because the bridge was packed with early morning Massgoers to the Cathedral. They looked on as the Fire Brigade and the lifeboat crews took the body from the water and placed her in the ambulance at the Fisheries Field.

Many of her classmates were sobering up from the celebrations when the news broke on Galway Bay fm that the body of a young woman had been taken from the River Corrib, but the name was not released which was just as well, as her family still hadn't noticed she hadn't come home. They were away for the weekend.
But her friends soon encountered sobriety when they heard the news and three Gardai were sent around to talk to them all in a bid to trace the last movements of Jessica. What they found out was mainly predictable. They'd been drinking in town in a few pubs but then they got take-outs and brought them down to the Spanish Arch where they sat along the grass and howled at the moon for a while and swore to always stay in touch when they went to college. They sat there and told each other that a special part of them was dying that night. The last they'd seen of Jessica was out on the Prom when she said that she had to get home because she was feeling sick and the others just sort of crashed out there on the concrete seats along the walk. When they woke up, she had gone, but then everyone was a bit dazed and she could have been anywhere, so they didn't bother looking for her. Dawn was almost up on the Bay and it was time to go home.

Following the radio appeal for information about the sighting of Jessica on the Prom, Salthill Gardai got a call from a woman walking her dog who had met her earlier and asked her if she was alright, but the girl told her to fuck off and so she did, bringing the dog with her. From the photograph they had, the woman was sure it was Jessica she had met — at the end of the Prom, miles from Dangan and the river.

Nightmusic

The squad car had been out the Prom earlier that night and had seen a group of them heading out that way. They had also seen three or four of the usual members of the Wirepullers Club as they called them heading down past the diving tower at Blackrock, a well-known spot for a sexual rendezvous of a solo nature.

They made a few calls to some of the usual suspects and honorary life members of the club, but most of them denied they had been at the tower that night. And most of them hadn't. But Kevin Hanniffy had, because Fogarty and the others had seen his car parked alongside the kerb. The Guards had given up going down to the tower now and lifting the lads who were lifting their lads. They hadn't had many complaints in recent months, but they knew it was still going on and anyway, the club members had co-operated in the conviction of a different case the previous year, so the guards let it be as long as they were discreet. And mainly they were.

Hanniffy worked in the town in the Civil Service, was single and had been brought in before when people complained that what was going on was disgraceful, grown men fumbling with themselves and each other, so he was used to defending his right to a seaside wank.

'I'll get my solicitor if you want to talk to me,' he said when Fogarty and Garda Catherine Kelly called to the door of his city centre apartment.

'No need for that, now. Are ya going to let us in?'

He led them into the living room.

'This is very nice. I'd say this costs ya a few bob, eh?' said Fogarty.

'I won't be harassed,' he said. Fogarty knew he was embarrassed with the female Garda there. He knew that he'd be more keen to co-operate in case Fogarty set out to really embarrass him.

'Arragh, cop on, for fuck's sake. This time you can genuinely be helping Gardai with their enquiries. You were at Blackrock the night before last.'

'Well, I might have...'

'Ya were, I saw your car.'

'OK, I went for a walk. But I...'

'Listen, I don't give a fuck for now what you're doing when ya go for a walk, just listen to me.'

He sat down opposite them.

'A young kid was drowned in the river that night. A Leaving Cert kid out celebrating. She was last seen walking out the Prom and now that's a fair stumble to make from the Prom to the River up past the Salmon Weir bridge.'

'What's this to do with me?' he said, standing up.

'You were at the Prom late, too. Now I'm asking you as a favour. Did ya see anything or anyone suspicious?'

'As a favour. Well,' he said sitting down again, more relaxed now that he knew he was not in any trouble himself.

'Town was crawling with them last night. They were everywhere. But it was quieter out at that end of the Prom. Some of them went down by the Golf Course and were drinking down there. But there was a girl, who was drunk and who had a row with a woman up on the Prom. She was there at the side of the road for a while. I think she was sick.'

'Did ya help her? Did ya go to see if she was alright?' said Garda Kelly.

'No, I didn't. I didn't know for sure. She was sick. Ya know, I couldn't just help her like that. If she screamed or anything, who would ya believe?'

'OK, go on,' she said.

'She wasn't there long though. She was thumbing.'

'Thumbing. At that hour of the night?' said Fogarty.

'Yeah, she nearly got knocked down a few times because she was walking onto the road. Then she came back in again and was leaning on the bonnet of a car.'

'So what happened to her then? Did she start walking home or what?'

'No, she went out in front of the next car that came along. I thought she was going to be hit by it, but it slowed down and she opened the door and got in. Fell in, more like. I think she knew the driver or something because she wasn't long getting in. And then they drove off.'

'Did ya get a look at the car?'

'Yes, it was a sort of a van. Dark coloured.'

Fogarty sat up in the chair.

'Could it have been green?'

'It could, but I couldn't be sure'

* * * *

Nightmusic

Melanie Whelan wondered if it was true about the oysters. She'd just had seven and she still wasn't feeling that randy. Just a bit sick. She'd have liked to go over to one of the many red faced revellers who had been feeling her every time she moved through the crowd in the marquee to go to the bar, and puke up onto their suits, but maybe they'd be flattered by the attention. She remembered Jack, her ex, telling her not to eat anything from the sea because fish piss in it.

Seven oysters. Jesus, but you had to take them and swallow. The men loved watching that, the swallow bit and the dribble out of the mouth. It's what the event was all about, drinking, eating, groping and then for ten minutes they'd watch some poor eejit open as many oysters as he could before they'd get back to drinking, eating and groping again.

She wondered had she counted right and had she really had seven? Maybe you had to have the full dozen for the effect to sink through. To be part of the crowd. To lose all sense of decorum and dignity. She took another sip of her wine. That was it. These were meant to be consumed with Guinness, large quantities of it. She looked across at the fat man with the red face who was slipping back the oysters as if he was putting in false teeth. Each salty slide down his throat was followed by a mouthful of stout. And a belch. It looked for all the world like a video of a man vomiting being shown backwards. She needed some fresh air. It was stuffy there in the tent, even if it was perched right on the edge of the river and beside the Spanish Arch. The instant she left the tent she felt better, the cool breeze that blew in over the Claddagh made her light skirt flap gently against her legs.

'Not slippin' up town for some shopping, I hope,' said the voice from behind her.

She looked around. It was Amy Cantwell. Amy had worked with her in Passion Public Relations in Dublin for some time before Melanie went off to set up her own company.

'Howya, Amy. No shopping, even though I wouldn't mind. Just the smell of farts and fags gets to me now and again. Fancy a stroll?'

'Why not? Why not? This will go on for a while yet anyway.'

If ya hadn't been told they were PR women, and hadn't heard their ridiculously PR-ish names, you'd have soon guessed anyway. If it wasn't the immaculately coiffed blonde hair that gave them away, it would have been the smart fitting suits that were at variance with the ill-fitting cocktail dresses the female guests were forever falling out of.

They emerged from the marquee into the sunset that threw a yellowish tinge on the walls of the Arch. They passed out by the statue to celebrate Christopher Colombus's visit to Galway, even though the shaggin' thing had been desecrated with so many bolts and nuts, it was hard to know what the original looked like. They made their up towards Jurys' before heading back out along the Long Walk.

'Aren't these buildings fucking desperate? How did they ever build them here with all this history around?'

'I don't know, I really don't know,' said Melanie. She wanted to ask Amy what the fuck she knew about history and what the fuck she knew about architecture. And PR, well that was another issue.

Privately, the two women hated each other. They'd been catty since the first day they met and things hadn't been helped by the fact that both of them had gone for the Oyster Fest PR job and both of them missed out on it.

But there was always next year. A contract like that is worth about £45,000, so they had to come to Galway, press the flesh, smile at the red faces and try to tear strips off the agency who got this year's contract. Discreetly, of course.

They turned left, took off their shoes and walked on the grass that led out to the Long Walk.

'I couldn't be arsed coming here next year. Same old fuckers, bulging bellies and massive arses all rutting against each other,' said Amy.

'And the men aren't any better,' said Melanie.

'But we'll be here and maybe one of us will be really working instead of pitching for a contract.'

'Did you ever think about moving down here permanently and setting up base in Galway?'

'Yeah, but there isn't great demand for it down here. Too much word of mouth and a design company every twenty yards. No, PR hasn't really caught on in Galway yet.'

'Well, maybe we'll change their minds then. Let's drink to that,' said Mel as she leaned over to click her glass off Amy's but as she did, the glass fell from her hand and onto the stone edging on the river walk, the glass shattering into the water and the red wine temporarily staining the blue.

'At least the oysters will be happier tomorrow after getting a mouthful of that.'

'Fuck, if the swans take a bit of that glass, blood will be spraying out of their necks like a garden sprinkler. Could be quite a sight, eh, Mel?

Tarantino does *Swan Lake.*'
But Mel wasn't laughing. Her eyes were staring at the water where the splinters were sinking.

The screams weren't heard in the tent because the jazz band were just belting out *Summertime* at the exact time she saw the face in the water. Bobbing away, bloated and staring at the sky.
Three or four others who saw the two women in suits screaming wondered if they were just pissed, but when the screams continued, they came over and spotted the body as well. The buckled legs hitting against the side of the pier with the movement of the tide, one bent back at an unbelievable angle. Two of the security men in the tent came down when they saw the commotion, quickly followed by their supervisor.
'Get back to the tent,' he told the uniforms. 'Keep the fuckin' music going and don't let this get out yet,' he said as he rang for the Guards. 'We need the full weekend.'
In Galway, everyone is on a contract.

* * * *

Nightmusic

The guards had great time for Malachy Lee. They called him out in the dead of night whenever there was something needed fishing out of the docks. A dog or a body or a car, or whatever, it didn't matter, he was always obliging. They'd find him in The Harbour or down at his boat or up in the library in the Hynes Building, and bring him down to help the Fire Brigade in the days before the Lifeboat got so sophisticated with their high tech boats and lights and radars and other shit. He was there the evening they took the old wan out of the canal. She was red rotten when they got her and put her in the coffin, but the coffin lid came off as the firemen were putting her away and the corpse fell out on the fireman. He laughed at that. They all did and had a cup of tea together afterwards back in the station on Fr. Griffin Road.

Malachy was very obliging. There were plenty of blokes who had boats on the river, but they weren't willing to give something back to the city. No, they just wanted to be on the water and show off and let on they weren't scared of the waves, but Malachy knew the Corrib tides and how they could be vicious bastards if you crossed them. The Guards knew as well that they were wasting their time trying to rouse one of the yacht or sailing crowd at night. They had no real fuckin' interest in the river apart from posing.

Often there'd be a report that someone had fallen off O'Brien's Bridge and there wouldn't be much time to get the lifeboat out, but Malachy would always be there before them anyway. He just had to be told where to go in the water and he'd manage to bring his 19-foot boat there, no matter how strong the current. And no matter how many jars he had, he was always willing to help the Guards.

Last Christmas, he was on the river when a young fella ran away from the guards and jumped into the water up at other end, near the canal. He tried to make it to the far side but nearly got himself drowned. He clung to the pillars in the middle of the river until Malachy came out with the guards in the boat and got him back on land, where the guards gave him a kick in the hole before arresting him.

He was great the time the college canoeing team got stuck there, all these international canoeists crying when they were pushed by the waves up against the gates of the Weir. Malachy got his wooden boat out to them and took them in one by one while holding the boat steady with one hand on the Mercury outboard motor. Oh, yes, there wasn't a

Nightmusic

gick out of them. Fuck all good their medals were to them then. Crying like babies they were, but he got them all in and when they said thanks, he just grunted back at them.

Every year, Superintendent Quigley rang him up to thank him for his help and to invite him along to the Galway Arms for the Christmas Drink. And Malachy always turned up, as he liked to be seen with the Gardai. He liked to be seen as someone who was important around town. He wanted to have his picture on the *Advertiser* instead of the guys from the lifeboat and the yachting club, but that never happened. Yet it might someday. But moments like this were great and made up for all those late nights of getting the boat out to help the good citizens of the city.

And now they were calling him out again. A body had been found in the Claddagh and they needed some help in getting it out. The lifeboat was already out around Aran trying to winch some wind surfer to safety. He told the Guard that he'd be there with the boat in two minutes. As he drove there he wondered what it was. He hoped it was a man. A man is handy. It takes the pressure off him a bit. There was no need to do one himself then. No need to fuck some poor bastard in just because you had to keep up the idea that Galway was suicide capital. And if you threw in the odd fella, then you could take a girleen yourself, and bring her to the cellar in the shed. There was nothing to be gained from the men. I mean, it's hard to toss off to them. If the river didn't give him a male body, he'd have to do one himself and there was always a lot of hassle involved. They were always strong bastards so they were, so you'd have to get them when they were drunk.

He remembered the time he got a student down around the back of the courthouse. He was a young fella having a piss into the river, would ya believe it? He was singing, or humming it was, Malachy remembered that. Before he knew it, he had crept up behind him, grabbed him and flung him towards the edge into the swirling froth that made its way at speed towards the sea. The young fella managed a shout but it didn't last too long as he entered the water head first and never righted himself. Malachy was worried about that one for a few days because he hadn't put your man's flute back in and that would look a bit suspicious. He thought about it for a few minutes as he watched the hand reaching out through the dark water before disappearing under the Salmon Weir bridge.

And the following few days when he helped in the search for the young man, he loved hearing the guards speculating about the reasons for the deaths, and how the victims had shown little signs of depression or craziness. They told him how the families had reacted and how the pathologist said this and the pathologist said that. They told him these things because they trusted him. After all, he was one of their friends, someone they turned to when they needed help. Nobody else asks him for help but the Gardai do, so maybe in the great scheme of things what he was doing may not be that wrong at all.

But still there was no point in trying to explain it to them.

They'd never really understand.

By the time Malachy got to the docks, the sub-aqua guys were there, had taken the body out, and put it in a coffin which was taken away in a hearse to the hospital. A crowd had come out from the oyster party and watched before being moved away by the Gardai. Malachy came down the river in the wooden boat and watched as the rubber dinghy did what he used to do, only much quicker. They had all the gear. Now there were too many people able to fish out bodies. Once there was only himself and the Gardai. Now the Fire Brigade, the Lifeboat and the sub aqua guys were doing it. Maybe the Gardai wouldn't be calling on him as often anymore. He turned the engine and headed back out around the mouth of the river. The Garda who rang him was now standing at the edge of the pier, but he didn't even wave or acknowledge Malachy. He didn't even say thanks or 'Sorry I got ya out at this hour of the evening' or 'I'll get ya a pint in the Arms when I clock off.'

Bastard.

* * * *

Nightmusic

At the morgue, the clothes were cut off the corpse and searched for any identification. All that was found was a Pass Card. Within a few minutes, Bank of Ireland had given the Gardai a home address for Kevin Jordan, and Westport Gardai were sent to Kilmovee to tell his parents and get a Galway address for the 19-year-old. His parents had only heard once from their son since he had gone to Galway to get a house for his second year in college. He rang last week to say he'd gotten someplace and gave them a number that could only take incoming calls. The fact that he hadn't rung much didn't bother them. Kevin was a bit odd like that. But Eircom were able to use the number to get an address and within fifteen minutes Noel Fogarty and Garda Catherine Kelly were around at the door. It didn't take them long to find what they were looking for. A white envelope on the kitchen table, addressed to Tony Jordan, the young man's father. Fogarty took it and read it out to Kelly as she moved around the kitchen looking for any signs of a disturbance.

'Dear Dad and Mam
I'm sorry for doing this to you, but it's the best option. First let me say that I love you all and that I'll probably be despised for what I'm doing. I hope this does not have too much effect on Shauna and Caroline. Tell them that they should aim to be better children than I managed to be. It was so hard to be a son to you. Sometimes the perfect son is unable to meet the requirements of the perfect father. Medication cannot cover the cracks in my life. Expectations are never all realised and can ultimately lead to disappointment, and that is the road I was taking, I fear. If you did not get this news now, you would get it later. I am sick Dad and Mam, and I do not want to waste away like a freak. I am not afraid of death, but I am afraid of dying. Please love me and my memory and let me go. Pray for me and free me to an existence where I can be what I once was, fit and healthy and fun-loving. For me it will be a release from the shackles of my current 'life.'
Goodbye. I love you
Kevin'

Fogarty ran his hand through his hair.
'D'ya hear that? For fuck's sake. Perfect fuckin' English. A brain box, I'd say that was what he was, and then he goes and does that to himself.'
'Steady on, Noel,' said Garda Kelly, clicking her fingers for him to hand

over the letter. 'Are we supposed to have read this? It's not for us.'
'This is an investigation into a death. It's evidence for the time being. It becomes a letter later.'
'Oh, right.'
'But what a waste. Too fuckin' bright these young lads are. There's no point learning young fellas if all they end up doing is writing great suicide letters.
I've seen some suicide letters in the past and they were shite. Ya couldn't make out any sense out of them but this fella seems to have been a bit of a brain box, even though it's fuck all good to him now, isn't it?'
He passed the note over to Kelly, who took it and read it quickly.
'Awful sad though, isn't it? Imagine what was going through his mind when he wrote this.'
But Fogarty was having none of it.
'Going through his mind, is it? I know what was going through his mind, fucking ecstasy or shit like that.'
'Oh Noel, these suicides are not all drugs related, ya know. People are genuinely depressed. He was sick or something.'
'Depressed, huh. A kick in the hole is what they want. If he could write letters this good he shouldn't be killing himself. That's not depressed. That's just fuckin' stupid. Be honest, ya have to agree, haven't ya?'

Catherine didn't like this side of Fogarty. He wasn't that old that he should be spouting out all this venom. She had enough of that from the old Guards at first, like Garda O'Toole who ended most conversations with 'Don't worry. It could be worse, the baby could be black.' And another day, he said that some fella in town had shacked up with some young wan and left his wife because the stomach was gone in her.
She knew that Fogarty had the dark side into which he lapsed from time to time, when he'd display amazing humanity, and then other times, he'd want to kick the shit out of everybody, like knackers and queers and emigrants. She felt scared when he spoke like this. Now he had that black look in his face again, the one he gets when people cross him. She knew too that there was no point continuing the conversation because he was going to be right whether he was or not. And you just had to accept it. So they went back to the Station with the note to give it to SuperQuigley, but he'd already left for UCHG where the postmortem was already being carried out.

Nightmusic

'Why don't ye give me some decent murders any more? All I'm getting are suicides and car crashes and the likes. Nothing to keep one at the forefront of one's profession,' said Dr. Greene.

The Super smiled at the aging pathologist.

'Did ya every think of going for the big job in Dublin, with John Harbison and his crew? They're short staffed aren't they and there's always a good run of suspicious deaths.'

'What? Go to Dublin and miss out on the fine golf and fishing in the west? You must be joking, Superintendent. Go to Dublin. Huh. Dublin is the cancer of this country. It is the primary and its effects are the secondary. If this country goes to the dogs, you can be sure that its problems will have emanated in Dublin. Just look at your main concerns and see which of them originated in the west. OK, take away the petty land squabbles and the drunken fighting, but the serious problems — the drugs and the armed robbery — they are all gifts from our capital city. They are the only things which are truly being decentralised on an equitable basis. We are bringing these in upon ourselves.'

'Arragh now Doctor, there are lots of fine people in Dublin, too. I was there for a while as a young Garda and they were the finest...'

'Yes, Superintendent, the people are fine, but some groupings of them have gone beyond humanity. Many of the people walking around Dublin may as well be from another planet. They have different motivations...'

'Ah come on now, ya can't say that about them...'

There was a short squelch as Greene took out the brain and plopped it into a dish and then placed the dish on the scales, and carried on talking.

'OK, maybe I'm being too cruel. but they did steal my car some years ago...'

'Who?'

'Dublin gurriers. But I'm not bitter and twisted about it,' he said grinning.

'To answer your questions though, no, I have no intention and never have had of leaving the west to go to Dublin. Galway is just about as much as I need even though it would be nice to have some interesting deaths from time to time.'

'My job is to prevent them, Doctor, not line them up.'

'Ah yes, Superintendent Quigley, but that is not within your control.

You are, unfortunately for your sake, the conduit of bad news. You are the middleman of misfortune. You are there, and so am I. Right there at the cutting edge of each tragedy. What is that line? 'Listen to the sirens wail, some go to emergency, others go to jail.'

'Is that poetry? I'm not into poetry, meself,' said Quigley.

'No, it's a pop song by Don Henley. Of the Eagles. You must remember The Eagles.'

'Oh, right. The Eagles. Maybe you're right, but I'd still prefer not to have any deaths on my patch. The job is hard enough without having to deal with murders.'

The Super hated the way Dr. Greene listened to what he had to say and then spouted out his own opinions as if what the Super had said didn't matter at all. As if he really thought that someone who went to Templemore could have something interesting to pass on to someone who went to the Royal College of Surgeons. He was a nice man, Dr. Greene, but he talked a lot of shite, too.

He had the preliminary report faxed over about an hour after he scrubbed up. While SuperQuigley ripped it off the machine, Doctor Greene was teeing off at the first in the Galway Bay Golf Club, his work done for the day.

The report stated what he had said when the body came in. Death was caused by asphyxia as a result of drowning. There was water, dirty water in the lungs and airways, and the young man's last meal was something like a pizza. There were no suspicious marks on the body. There were two scars, one for an appendix operation and another for a knee operation...

But there was still something fishy about the whole thing. There were just too many bodies floating out in the bay or popping up in the Corrib. Quigley didn't give a fuck if this was the fastest growing city in Europe or not. All he knew was that there were people dying now who should not be dying. Young people who were flinging themselves into the waves. Or was it as simple as that? He looked at the fax again and read the cause of death. He knew Greene would have spotted it if there had been anything suspicious.

Quigley had looked at so many of these reports in recent months, but still he looked closely at the wording of the cause of death and at the reports that had been taken from the two women who found the body. Jesus, Greene had said he was looking for a suspicious death and not these run of the mill drownings again. So he'd have been that extra bit vigilant in case there were some discrepancies. But there didn't seem to be. And now Fogarty and Kelly were back with the note from the house. And the young man's father had said that young Kevin had been in trouble a few times and that suggested that there was nothing fishy about it at all. But it still didn't seem right.

There was a knock on his door.

It was Fogarty. The first time he'd been here since the ballscratching incident. SuperQuigley hadn't forgotten that and didn't ask him to sit down.

'Can I have a word, sir?'

'Yes, Noel. What is it?'

'This death, sir. It's a suicide.'

'How perceptive, Noel. But there is a note.'

'No, sir, I mean that I think this is a suicide precisely because there is a note, but the others are still very vague. Are you happy, sir that foul play is not suspected to any extent in these deaths?'

'What are you suggesting, Fogarty?'

'I know, sir, you might think I'm speaking out of turn and all that, and the city is a crazy place full of crazy fuckin' bastards, excuse my French, sir, but is there some reason why nine or ten people have killed themselves in the river this year so far? I was thinking there might be some reason behind it.'

'Such as...'

'Such as a cult or something, sir, or drugs.'

'I appreciate your thinking Noel, but there is nothing to suggest any link between them, at all. It's a sign of the times, Noel. People are killing themselves all the time, but I don't think there is anything to connect them at all. And neither do the lads down in the Detectives Room or the drugs squad. Most of these people who have done this have some form of odd streak in them...'

'Patrice Nolan, sir?'

'Well, she was a bit flirty wasn't she? For an 18-year-old. She had run away from home before and she was, ahem, promiscuous.'

'But with respect, sir.'

'Garda Fogarty, listen. Bring me the evidence of a link between any two. Just two and we'll consider it. OK? I don't mean to be abrupt now, but I've had a heavy day, ah, like yourself.'

* * * *

Nightmusic

Morley was in the planning office of the County Council on Prospect Hill when the call came from Fogarty. It was something he had to do every second Monday to see if there were any unusual planning applications in. He left down the file he was looking at and went out into the sunlit foyer of the new building to answer the call.

'David.'

'Noel Fogarty here. Can ya talk?'

'Yeah.'

'Listen, you've got to give me a hand. There was another body...'

'Where?'

'In the docks. Some birds at the Oyster festival found it. Nearly fuckin' shit themselves. Fire Brigade and the sub aquas dragged him out. A fella. A student from Mayo.'

'Right, so is there something strange about it?'

'Well, he's a geansai.'

'A wha?'

'A fuckin' geansai. A jumper. A suicide.'

'Aw, right.'

'He left a note so he did it all right, but I'm wondering if he was in any cult or anything. Said he was sick. There's too many fuckin' bodies. I spoke to himself upstairs but I might as well have been talkin' to me bollocks.'

'Was he interested at all?'

'Naw, told me to find evidence and then he'd entertain me. Fucker. So can ya start looking at cults and things in the area. Ya had something about them before. Jehovah's witnesses and the likes.'

'They're not cults, they're religions.'

'Still, I wouldn't fuckin trust them shower of arse bandits.'

'Right, I'll check them out so but they don't kill themselves. You're lookin' at crowds like the Moonies and the screamers...'

'Right. Whatever. Just find out what ya can and give me a shout. And remember when you win your bloody Cross Biro Journalist of the Year, you'll be thanking me.'

'Hang on, what about...'

But Fogarty had hung up.

And Morley went back to checking why people fight over land.

When Morley got home, he spent the whole evening looking for information on cults. He tried the Internet but all it spewed out were details of groups which were based in Canada. He went through all the search engines, Yahoo, Webcrawler, HotBot, Alta Vista, the lot, but still the only stuff coming up was about Waco and Jim Jones and a rake of others he didn't really care about. There didn't seem to be anything connecting them to Ireland at all. And anyway, none of them actually proclaim suicide as being one of the mandatory conditions for membership, so where do ya start? He rang Emily Hogan who did work from time to time with the *Irish Catholic* and other Holy Joe papers and who had a degree in theology. She faxed him a list of the groups operating in the country. But the only ones operating out of the west were harmless enough divils, prayer groups and loonies living in converted caves in Connemara or Sligo. He searched through the websites from the regional newspapers and found nothing on cults or groups like that, but lots on suicide.

He wondered what motivated a guard like Fogarty. What was he going to gain from something like this? Even if this came off and he discovered a link between them all, he wasn't surely going to get promotion or anything. This was Galway, not Hollywood, and Fogarty was no Frank Serpico. He typed Fogarty's name into the search engine for the crack and surprisingly it came up several times, mostly on court reports in the Galway newspapers. But there was an article about how he ran into a blazing house to save a kid, and how he was given a Scott medal for bravery for that. And another on how he saved a man from drowning in the Corrib and was given a bravery citation by the Corporation. He wondered if the man had been a geansai as well and had he wanted to drown but Fogarty stopped him. He wondered a lot about Fogarty, and how he wouldn't like to cross him on a dark night. He tried again for suicide statistics and printed them out.

In the end, he just flicked through his e-mails, checked the newsgroups he had subscribed to, took a look at the chicken house website which was a voyeur site focused on a group of naked Asian girls living in a house in Tokyo. But even Ping Li and Kitty Won must have been bored as well, as they were all gone to bed. So he decided to do the same thing.

But just as he was leaving the room and knocking off the light, there was a tap on the window which made him jump. He didn't know who it could be at this hour. He pulled back the curtains and a red face peered in through the glass.

Nightmusic

It was Fogarty.
'Are ya letting me in?'
'Sure.'
'You were on your computer.'
'I was. I was looking for some stuff.'
Fogarty was in his civvies — his blue jeans and grey fleece top. He came in and sat down on the chair looking at the screen just as it was shutting down.
'I'd say that cost ya a lot. A thousand or so, but aren't ya cleaning up on the stuff for the papers? I see the stuff ya write in the tabloids. Awful shite. Half of it isn't fuckin' true. Who's this anonymous Garda spokesperson you're always quoting? I'd say you're makin' half of it up.'
Morley didn't disagree. What was the point?
'Cup o' tea or a can of Budweiser?'
'Jaysus, I often drank a can o' tea. In the bog like. Bud will be grand. Let it go, Louis.'
'What?' said Morley.
'Louis, the fuckin' lizard. Jaysus, I love them ads. Especially the one where the lizard is swearing revenge on the frogs and yer man says "Let it go, Louis, let it go." I use that phrase a lot. It comes in handy down below in the station. There's a fella called Louis there, ya see.'
'Oh, right. I found your name on the Net.'
'What? What was I in it for?'
'The papers are all in here, so every time your name was in the paper, it got placed onto the website.'
'Is my picture in there?'
'No, just stuff about your court appearances, and your medal and the Corpo thing for jumping in the river.'
'Corpo thing for jumping in the river. Ya mean my citation for bravery. Fuckin' cheek of ya. Corpo thing for jumping in the river.'
'Well, ya know what I mean. I never knew ya were a decorated hero. Let me bow.'
But then Morley realised that it was not sensible to pull the piss out of Fogarty. He could be all lightness and smiles one minute and the next he'd have your balls by the hand, so he let it go.
'I got that because some fella tried to kill himself and I went in after him. He started hitting me and told me to fuck off, but I dragged him ashore and he went in again, so the second time I went in, I kneed him in the balls and he was very passive then.'

Nightmusic

'Well, the upshot of it all,' said Fogarty, 'is that there's fuck all to go on. Is there anyone you could talk to about these deaths? Will the Super not talk to ya at all?'
'No, I'm not flavour of the month. This year.'
Fogarty opened the can and even though it did not fizz, he still managed to spill some of it on the couch. Morley didn't mind. The place was rented, and so was the couch.
'Would the Lifeboat talk to me about it or the Fire Brigade?'
'I don't know, I think they're in the same boat as us, pardon the pun, they can only speak through one person.'

Morley switched on the computer again and showed Fogarty his name on the net.
And the names of a few other guards he typed in.
And the GAA website and the betting one.
And the on-line auction for used cars.
And the FBI Most Wanted List.
He didn't bother showing him the Chicken House one because in terms of morality you never know where ya stand with guards. You could be having the crack with them and thinking anything goes, but next thing they'd turn on ya, so he decided to play safe and stick to the safe websites. No point showing a guard a toss-off website. In their world, every man should be getting some and if he wasn't, then he was to be watched.
Fogarty was fascinated.
'We're learning this shit, ya know, down the station. It's called Pulse and we have to go to classes from next month to learn it properly. It'll be great when it's up and running, even though the way I am with computers I'll probably wipe the whole fuckin' thing by mistake some night I'm on me own down in Mill Street.'
He finished the can in a few slugs and got up to go.
'Nice place ya have here. For Tuam, like. How much would ya be paying for a place like this?'
'Enough. Enough, like.'

And then he was gone, promising he'd get a few names of people who might be able to talk about the bodies in the river. Social workers and psychologists and the likes around Galway who the station use from time to time.

'I'd e-mail a list of the names to ya. If I had e-mail. And a fuckin' computer,' he said. Then he grinned and disappeared into the darkness from whence he had come.
And Morley really went to bed.

* * * *

Nightmusic

Gerry Healy secured the trolley back into its place at the back of the catering carriage. The train had left Athenry and would be in Galway in thirteen minutes, so there'd be just enough time for a fag with Tommy Sherry. He'd just been working on the train for the summer and then when school started again, he just didn't feel like going back. He loved it though, pushing the trolley up and down the carriages, selling coffees and muffins.

Except at the weekend. He hated the weekends because then all the thick GAA fans would be on, roaring for drink and chips, and asking him who the fuck did he think he was pushing his trolley on the aisle of the carriage they had paid a ticket for. He hated the Special trains and the GAA fans and their Special tickets. He wanted to ask them if they ever thought what the word Special said about them, but he didn't because he liked the job. And he liked his teeth where they were.

But just as he put the fag to his lips, there was a smack, a kind of loud slap and the train jolted slightly. Tommy looked out the window.

'What the fuck was that?'

'Dunno.'

'Must have been a stone or a plank.'

'Plank, me hole. That was a cow or something,' said Tommy. 'I was on a train once when we hit a cow. He was splattered all over the front of the train and with the speed we were going, we could have had steaks fried on the engines.'

'Oh, that really wants to make me eat on the trains now, doesn't it? I hope we're not delayed, though. I'm meeting Yvonne in the Quays at ten.'

'Stall on, you'll be all right. Let's go and have a gander.'

As they spoke, the train slowed down on the Galway side of Oranmore. People who had been reaching up for bags and rucksacks got up to stand in the aisle, thinking they were in Galway, but a quick look out the window and the darkness told them they weren't. So they sat down again, feeling ridiculous with all their coats and bags gathered up, and smiled at each other.

The two drivers were the first to come out, and go back the line with their torches and spot the mass of blood and entrails that stuck out from underneath the train. One of them was throwing up as Martin and Tommy came along, their cigarettes still in their mouths.

'Is it a cow? It's a cow isn't it?' said Tommy to the driver who wasn't

Nightmusic

puking.
'No, Tommy lad, cows don't wear runners,' the other driver said.
They looked down at the two legs stuck under one of the metal wheels and then the two lads puked.

It was the Fire Brigade who found the other half. They're always called for the dirty jobs. There might not be a fire for miles, but if there's any bit of decapitation to be cleaned up, or guts to be hoovered, the Fire Brigade get the call. 'You make 'em, we scrape 'em' should have been their motto. But this one was a bit awkward. Jammed in under one of the wheels and there was no way the train could move without splicing it further.
But when they looked inside, they could see they were only dealing with half a body, so at least that was something.

It didn't take them long to find the upper half of the body. It was lodged in some bushes by the side of the track down a bit further. The whole thing was a right mess, but they reckoned it was the body of a woman. In her fifties or more. Now what was she doing walking along the railway line after dark?

* * * *

SuperQuigley could not believe it. This was the tenth body to be discovered this summer. He reckoned he should have a seat reserved for him here at the pathologist's office.

'When I asked ya to bring me a suspicious death, you could have been a wee bit tidier, Superintendent,' said Greene.
'Two halves. Jesus, what more can you ask for?'
Greene was in great form. He'd won the medical association fourball with his mates from the hospital, and the celebrations had gone on into the night.
The halves of the body were on separate slabs and he kept going from one to the other.
'I think we can safely say that death occurred as a result of massive haemorrhaging, consistent with an impact such as being hit by a train. That of course is just a really preliminary finding, and not one I needed to go to college for seven years to arrive at. The more intricate results

Nightmusic

will have to come later.'
'Right. We think we might know her. She's one of those who drinks in the Square. So she might have been drunk as well, and wandered out there from the homeless shelter.'
'Indeed she might, Super and I will do my utmost to ascertain what she had consumed before she made that fateful walk. What's the Johnny Cash song? 'I Walk The Line.' That's one for the Hospital Requests programme to get for this poor lady.'
SuperQuigley didn't laugh but took his cap and left.

Morley had all the details about two hours after the discovery. The father of a friend of his worked in the Fire Brigade so the news soon filtered back to him. He told the friend that every Fire Brigade story he got him would be worth two or three pints to him. And this was a beaut. Talk about gore. Train to the west. Woman sliced in two. Distressed passengers, even if they didn't see anything. All the ingredients of a page lead for the tabloids.
But one of the down sides of sending late night stories from the west to the tabloids is that their Irish desks have shut for the night, and you have to deal directly with the English sub-editors in London. And as most of these have never heard of the West of Ireland, they ring until near midnight asking for spellings of this and spellings of that, names, and ages and what colour was the dog and what did they have for breakfast and the likes.
The story had only been e-mailed over about ten minutes when the first one came from *The Sun*.

'Now that's an interesting death,' Tristan the subbie in London told Morley. 'Two halves.'
'Can you tell me where the break was?'
'Sorry?'
'The break. The cut. In the body. Where was it?'
Morley had to think. He hadn't asked the Gardai, but in cases like this it was better to bullshit.
'Around the stomach.'
'Sorry.'
'The middle. The groin, the waist, you know, clean cut. Even Steven. Two good halves.'
'OK. Now how do you spell the station again in Galway?

'Ceannt. C E A N N T.'
'Not cunt,' laughed Tristan.
'No, Ceannt.'
'Cunt station would not be so inviting, would it?'
'No, not really,' said Morley, thinking it might give 'going down to Galway for the weekend' a whole new meaning.
'And the name of the train company?'
'Iarnrod Eireann.'
'As in iron rod, is it?'
'No, not exactly.'
'Funny that, iron rod and cunt, isn't it?'
'Yeah, it's hilarious.'
'Do you want your name on this? Your byeline?'
'Don't care, Tristan. As long as me byeline is on the cheque.'

Despite the lateness of the hour, all the papers said they'd take the story. Six papers, one story, the same story, one e-mail and six cheques, many of them sterling.
Not bad for a wet Tuesday night.

* * * *

Nightmusic

Malachy watched it all from the boat. He didn't use an engine to move out from the shore. He checked his watch to see what time the train was due and it was not too late, just a few minutes past its due time when he saw the lights of the carriages as it snaked its way around the coast, leaving Oranmore and Rinville and moving in the sort of slow way it does towards Galway City. He didn't hear the noise of the impact. That would have been a bonus, but he was too far out to hear anything, and anyway he had his tape recorder playing *Cosi Fan Tutte* just as Wolfgang would have liked it, to be heard over a sheet of water with no obstacles. However, the train stopped fairly suddenly, so he knew it must have happened.

'Fuckers. That'll show them,' he said to himself out loud, without realising it.

They should never have treated him the way they did. He used to be The Man. The one they used and now they were using all the highfangled crowd, the divers and the lifeboats and they never said a word of thanks or a sorry for humiliating him in the way they had. He felt a right prick that evening in the river in his wooden boat while the divers crowd were there with their bright orange rubber dinghy and enough gear to raise the Titanic. He should have been treated better. Well, if they wanted bodies and wanted to use the professionals then he'll give them bodies. Let them get a bit of practice in if they want to be good at it. He hadn't expected to go fishing that evening, but sometimes you come upon a shoal that you just cannot leave behind. Fish are like that. You never know when they're there, but the best fishermen are always on the alert for one, always on their guard, just as he had been that evening when he saw her, the auld bitch.

He hadn't tossed off to Bridie Maloney at all. But then again, ya wouldn't would ya, the state of her? He saw her down at the back of St. Patrick's Avenue just off the Square. He had been in to say a prayer in St. Patrick's and there she was sprawled in a corner, sitting on an anorak at the back of the old church. He parked the van there from time to time when he was in town. He went over to her to see if she was alive or dead. Bridie was in her fifties now, was always drunk, but she knew him.

'Malachy Lee, what are ya doing here? Give us a few bob for a drink.'
'Bridie, how are ya? You're still on the tear, are ya?'
'Arragh, what d'ya think? How's your mother?'

Nightmusic

'Grand. Getting auld, like us all.'
'Tell her I'm sorry about that china dog. I didn't mean to ... Are ya still doing the mackerels and the likes?'
'A bit of this, a bit of that. Whatever's going, ya know?'
'Well, are ya going to give me money for a drink?'
'I'll do better than that. I'll bring ya for a drink. I've the van here. Fancy a proper drink, rather than the piss in those bottles?'
He looked at the bottle she was holding.
'Chardonnay. Far from fuckin' Chardonnay you were reared. Did ya nick this, it's £6 a bottle?'
She didn't answer him, but got up and went towards the van.

She stank like hell and didn't say much to him in the car. She fell asleep a few times, then woke up at one stage and offered to pull his wire for him, but he told her not to bother. So she didn't. She said she wanted to get out somewhere around Furbo for a piss, but he was going too fast, and then she started to sing. He reached under the seat and took out the Baby Power, unscrewed the top and handed it to her.
'Bloody whiskey. Great stuff.' She let it back slowly. Not all at once, as he thought she would.
'Drink up, there's no one watching.'
So she did and started another when he got her to the shed and sat her there. When she thought she could take no more, he held open her mouth and put more in, but it came out her nose when she resisted it. She was muttering a lot and then she fell asleep. He looked at her closely. Her face was really rubbery and wrinkled and tanned. They were all tanned in the Square.
She used to be a great friend of Martin Kilkelly and came with him to the house years ago when he was bringing in turf, but she stole a china dog that Mother had on the mantlepiece, so Mother never let her back again. Kilkelly got the dog back alright for Mother, but she never forgave her. And now here she was in the same place Kilkelly ended up. Like all the others in the Square, Bridie was said to have been beautiful once, though it was hard to see how now. Her hair was grey and greasy and matted, she had the starting of a grey moustache and she was fat. He thought about opening the corduroy jeans she wore, for a look, but he was put off by the smell of her, so he didn't bother.

He reversed the van up to the door but this time he put her in the back

Nightmusic

and made the drive down to the boat. It was dark now, and he brought his torch. He dragged her into the boat, laying her on the floorboards underneath two of the seats. And beside the fishing rods and the feathers. Then he went back and got his tape recorder and the *The Music of Mozart* cassette that he got in a petrol station, then pushed himself out with the oars until he got into deep water. He turned on the engine and made his way across the bay to where the lights of the new hotel on the golf course shone out like a great ship in the night. It was cold on the bay tonight, but the boat rode cross wave and made good progress. He looked down at her, she was still asleep or unconscious. He had another bottle with him in case she woke up and got rowdy, but she didn't. And she still hadn't by the time he got to the shore near the army's rifle range. He put one arm under her, and dragged her across through the long grass, under the barbed wire fence, and up the stones to the track. There was a smell of fresh creosote off the beams under the steel tracks. He put her down again, opened her mouth a bit more and poured some more whiskey in. Then he opened her jacket to expose the wine bottle in her inside pocket. She was smaller than he thought, and her full body didn't reach from track to track, so out of respect for her, he placed her half across one track, so that at least her face wouldn't be ruined.

Then he wiped his hands and made his way back through the grass to the boat, rowed out, took a swig from the bottle he had brought and waited for the train to come. That'll teach them. Bodies. Let them clean up that mess. Let them get the divers for that, or the lifeboat.

'Let them sort that one out,' he said to himself as he took another drink, pushed the play button on the tape recorder, listened to Cosi Fan Tutte and watched as the line of lit carriages made their way in along the coast.

'Well, Watson, we can but possess our souls in patience and see what the hour may bring.'

* * * *

Nightmusic

The Garda Press Office gave Davy Morley the name of Bridie Maloney the following day, as there weren't too many family members to inform. Normally there is a twelve-hour wait before the names are released but then in this case nobody would be flying home from America for Bridie's funeral. Any family she had didn't want anything to do with her, since she had left the bosom of the family home thirty years earlier for the coldness of the alleys around Eyre Square. She was a great singer and sang in the musical society, taking the lead role in a few shows. Everyone in Galway said she could have sang on stage in the Royal Albert Hall, she was so good, but she drank instead, and gave up her chance of fame to emulate her heroines Judy Garland and Jayne Mansfield.

But getting the name at ten the following morning was little use to Morley because the papers would want to know more than that. It was too early to file copy as the papers would want the full details of what had happened, and how the auld wino had manage to get that far out the railway line. They wanted "a pick-up" which is a photo of a dead person, but that was a job for the photographer and not for Morley, so he rang a few snappers and told them to get around to the houses and see if they could find one. Getting a "pickup" is one of the dirtiest jobs in journalism as you never know how you are going to be received. In the case where you expect to be ran from the door, you're brought in and given tea while they select a nice photo from the sideboard, and in the houses where you expect a sympathetic hearing, you're told to fuck off. There weren't many photos to be had of Bridie though, as her family did not want any connection with her, even though she'd been sliced in two. But one of the photographers had her from the previous year's Christmas party for the homeless up at the computer factory and soon enough the image of Bridie Maloney was electronically whirring tis way to newspapers around the country. Her fifteen seconds of fame having come just too late for her, but at least in one sense she'd emulated Jayne Mansfield who was decapitated in a car accident in 1967.

One of the workers in the church said that he saw her in the grounds around five o'clock and she didn't look in any condition for a four-mile walk. This bothered the Super as well. And another thing was that Dr. Greene had said that she had consumed quite an amount of whiskey, although there was a Chardonnay bottle found broken in her inside

Nightmusic

breast pocket.

SuperQuigley rang the Commissioner in the Park and told him the details as far as he knew them. He had been on to the Commissioner many times that summer trying to get the fifty extra Gardai for the city, and the Commissioner had told him that the crime figures didn't warrant it. 'How about ten bodies? Does that fucking warrant it?' he felt like saying, but no, you had to be polite to your superiors in cases like this. But surely each dead body was worth an extra four or five Gardai. That would be 40 and that would keep everyone happy. He'd love to swing the extra Gardai for the city before he retired in ten years time but he knew too that despite the Commissioner's mantra, the decision had fuck all to do with crime figures and a lot to do with politics in the Department.

Fogarty heard about the train accident on the morning news on Galway Bay fm. He was late, so he just grabbed a slice of toast, slurped down a cup of tea and put on his tie while heading out the door.
He cornered Mike O'Donnell in the Pulse Room and asked him to do a check on all the green vans in the city and county.
'Green vans?'
'Yeah. Green vans?'
'Any particular shade of green, Garda Fogarty? Is it knackers you're after?'
'Could be. It could be.'
'There could be thousands of them. Big ones and small ones....'
'Which? Knackers or vans?'
'Vans.'
'And there might not. I need to find out something. Private job. Say nought and there's a pint in it for ya.'
'What if himself upstairs asks me what it's for?'
Fogarty caught O'Donnell by the cheek and shook it affectionately.
'Sure he knows fuck all about the system either. Baffle him with bullshit, Mike. Baffle him with bullshit.'

Fogarty was shocked when he heard it was Bridie Maloney who had been killed as he'd often stopped for a chat with her above in the Square.
He remembered that she stank of high heaven and that when he came to Galway first he used to be embarrassed if she called him over. He

knew that she was trying to make a fool out of him in front of her cronies there in the Square and he fell for it at the beginning, as did all the new young guards.

The last time he'd seen her, he was taking her out of one of the big department stores up town where she'd gone in and started spraying herself with the latest fragrance from Yves San Laurent. She told the immaculately coiffed assistant who had asked her to leave to go and fuck herself. Which she didn't. And that's why Fogarty had been called. As he took her by the arm and directed her outside, Bridie protested to him that the bottle had 'free sample' stamped on it, and that she was just as entitled as the next person to go in and try it for herself.

And Fogarty thought she had a point.

Yves Saint Laurent is fuck all good to her now, he thought, as her halves lay on the slab above in the hospital.

The Super called them back into the conference room just after their breakfast. He said that he was very concerned about the number of deaths which had not been fully cleared up in the city.

'Now while there may be a good and valid reason for every single one of them, we cannot close the file until we are sure that that is the case, do ya follow me, men? And women, of course. The death of Bridie Maloney last night was probably an accident, but if that is the case, we don't want it to happen again, so I want ye to talk to the organisations for the homeless and others who may be able to ascertain why Miss Maloney was that far out the line at that hour of the night. She was believed to have consumed a large amount of whiskey and she had an empty wine bottle on her person, so can you ask around the off-licenses as well, ya know the ones that sell that crowd drink. Ask if she was buying that kind of stuff. This was a particularly gruesome death, and we have to tread carefully, before I make any further statement to the media on it. At the moment, it's being treated as an accident, but the circumstances of the accident are still under investigation. That's the line we're going on. OK, men. And women, of course. Again.'

Before Fogarty finished at 2 o'clock that afternoon, Mike O'Donnell was back to him with a list of green vans in the county. There were 987 vehicles of that description.

'Here's some bedtime reading for ya, Noel,' he said as he handed over the rolls of printout paper.

'Jaysus, that was quick.'
'Sure I'm only brilliant.'
'Ya know, Mike, you're like a blind whore. I have to hand it to ya.'
'Enough of the praise. I hope I get me pint as promptly as that.'
'The weekend Mike, the weekend. Fair play to ya, and remember, don't say a word to Superman.'

* * * *

Nightmusic

The grease had cut through the bottom of the bag and the chips fell onto the table, but Morley gathered them up and put them back into the punnet. This is the worst thing about fast food. Ya have to eat it fast because it goes cold fast as well. He ran to the fridge, grabbed a carton of milk, a big mug and went back to the sitting room where what would have to do as dinner tonight was sprawled on the coffee table. He flicked from channel to channel while making sure not to get grease on the remote control. He stopped at Eurosport where they were showing Sumo wrestling.

He wondered how come the really good stuff on Eurosport is on during the day, the goals of the week and the World Cup stories, but whenever you come home at night and are interested in watching it, there is only shite like Sumo wrestling on it. I mean, you can't even follow it because both of the wrestlers looked the same, two mountains of white flesh, four wobbling cheek buttocks and two thin thongs. He poured himself a mug of milk and drank it back.

Morley had been looking forward to biting into this fish burger all the way home, especially the one side of it where all the dressing and tartar sauce lay. He opened the box, tore off the first wrapper and then the second and he was just lifting it to his mouth when he heard the tap on the window. He looked up and saw Fogarty outside.

'Fuck,' he said and decided against taking a bite, so he left it down and went to the door.

'Jaysus, it's fuckin' freezin out. Is that the kettle I hear whistling in he distance for me?'

'Ye'll have to wait. I'm in the middle of dinner.'

Fogarty looked at the pile on the table.

'Ya call that dinner. What you need is...'

'Some peace and quiet.'

'No, a woman, A woman would never let you ate that sort of rubbish now, so she wouldn't. She'd have ya atin' proper food and making sure you were looking after yerself.'

'Yeah. Right.'

Morley took a bite as Fogarty continued.

'Yeah. I've seen the likes of you journalists, or even young guards living in flats for years and not atin' proper food, and the next thing they have ulcers or piles. Is that what the milk's for? Have ya an ulcer?'

'No, I just like milk, that's all.'

Nightmusic

'Hah, no-one likes milk. Did ya ever wonder what the first guy to milk a cow thought he was doing, did ya?'
'No.'
'Anyway, take it easy on the fast food because piles are a fuckin' terror so they are. They're a right pain in the hole,' said Fogarty collapsing with laughter back onto the couch.
'Listen, mammy, I'm trying to eat here. Can ya drop the anal disease bit for a while?'
'Right, sorry. Ate up. What are ya watching?'
'Sumo wrestling.'
'Sumo wrestling. That's the Japanese or Chinese thing, isn't it?'
He took the remote and turned up the sound, taking a chip from Morley's punnet.
'Jaysus, look at the arse on yer man. I'd say he walks away from a fair shite now.'
Morley got up and threw down the burger.
'Fuck, that's it. Here you can eat this burger. I'm getting a cup of tea. I'll get something proper and wholesome to eat after you've gone.'
Fogarty looked at him with surprise as he went into the kitchen.
'Are ya sure ya don't want it?' said Fogarty as he leaned over and picked at the chips, in ones and twos and then in great handfuls.
'I'll leave the burger. Ya never know where ya've been, ya see.'
Morley came back in with two teabags and dropped them into the pot.
'What about your ulcer?' he said as he saw Fogarty tuck in with gusto.
'Oh, guards don't get ulcers. It's built into our immune system in Templemore.'
'What are ya here for anyway?'
'Breakthrough and homework time, sonny. I've got a link between the deaths.'
'All of them?'
'No, two of them.'
'Two out of ten. What's the link? That someone dies?'
'No need to be sarcastic, now. There's a van. A green van. It was seen by the friends of Patrice Nolan, and Jessica Kelly was seen getting into it at the Prom.'
'So, where do we go from here. Van hunting?'
'Here,' said Fogarty reaching into his inside pocket and pulling out a roll of printout paper that spread out across the floor.
'What's this?'

Nightmusic

'Names and addresses of 987 green van owners in Galway city and county, so let's go through them and see if we can eliminate them. In the Nolan case, the people who saw the van thought it was a knacker's van, so lets scrub out any of the big vans, or the small vans, and concentrate on those in the middle. Remember the slogan 'ten thousand knackers can't be wrong, 'cos they all bought a Hiace von.'

Three hours later, they still hadn't gotten through them all. The Sumo wrestling had ended and now there was indoor skateboarding on. Morley's phone bill had taken a walloping too because of the calls that Fogarty made to colleagues around the county asking about owners and past histories and all of that.
To make it worse, every time he got through to a station, he enquired about the guard's family, how their kids were doing at school and what they thought of Galway's chances in the football the following year. Morley had visions of all the money he earned being spent on phone calls.
Fogarty attacked his hair with a pencil and threw down the sheet of paper.
'It's the Celtic Tiger that's ruining us. If there wasn't so much feckin' building going on, there'd be less vans. See there, 32 vans for companies of bricklayers, wirers, electricians, chippies. A few years ago those fellas would be pushing wheelbarrows over in London, but now we're booming, they're over here. With their own companies and their own vans. Take away the Celtic Tiger and it'd be only the knackers who'd have the vans.'
'Ya know,' said Morley, 'this reminds me of a Fás scheme I was on years ago when we were working on cleaning up a football pitch and were sent out picking stones in the carpark. Picking stones, would ya mind? You'd never finish that job.'
'Bit of a glass hammer and rubber nails jobs, those Fás schemes, I'd say,' said Fogarty.
'Yeah, they were but you see, this is like it. We're getting somewhere but we're not getting anywhere. This is totally laborious.'
'Hang on, look we've knocked two hundred off the list and it's getting smaller. Somewhere in there is the name of someone who's been at the scene of where two people have gone missing. That has to be something. I know if I went to the Super with this, he'd laugh his hole off, but we've got to keep trying. Listen if nothing comes out of it, we'll

Nightmusic

have something to laugh about, won't we? And I'll buy ya a pint.'
They made more tea, tore into it again and reduced the list further.
After that, they went onto the Internet on Morley's computer.
He went to the regional newspapers site and typed in "attempted abductions," and then added in the words "green van" to aid in the search. In a few minutes, it gave him a list of all the attempted child abduction incidents involving vans in the country. Most of these were white vans. There were a few red cars, but only three with a green van. And two of those were in Connemara about four years beforehand. He printed out the sheets and put them with the list of numbers and went and made even more tea.

Mary was in bed when Fogarty got back from Tuam around 3 am. He had mastered the knack of closing the doors in the house without making any noise. He threw his shirt into the wash basket and undressed out on the landing. He felt manky, but it was too late to have a bath at this hour, and it was too late for Elvis so he went in and had a shower instead after having a leak that seemed to last forever. In the shower, he lathered himself in shower gel, even his hair, and then turned the switch so that it would rinse off with cold water — the sharpness of it tearing at his head as he stood there braving it out.
He dried himself, put on his shorts, went over the window and looked out at the lights of the city — an orange arc in the sky stretching from Renmore to Salthill looking like some weird form of night rainbow caused by the neon streetlamps. Gosh, there were a lot of lights out there, even at this hour of the night. The city had gotten a lot bigger since he moved here and he knew almost every inch of it, but now there was something here that was alien to them all. Can a city get that big without having some form of evil in it? Somewhere beneath the happy picture of cultural capital and party town, there had to be a sub-level made up of some weirdos. There had to be. A city like this doesn't grow without stamping on people. He pulled the curtain back, and looked, and wondered if somewhere out here, there was a green van driven by some sad bastard.
And he wondered if that sad bastard had any inkling that they were getting that little bit closer to him.
And if he did, would it be in time to stop him killing again?

* * * *

Nightmusic

The post always arrived about ten o'clock, Normally it would be just a few letters or bills and they'd patter onto the floor, but whenever a parcel came, the postman would have to knock at the door and hand it in because the letter box was too small. Today, there was a knock. Malachy went to the door himself, rising up from the kitchen table and wiping the toast-crumbs off his chin and munching as he went. Mother hadn't heard the knock as usual and looked up to see why he'd left so suddenly. She watched as he came back through the hall, tearing at the paper which wrapped the package which had come this morning. Through the angle of the door, she could see him looking at it and then wrapping it again and leaving it on the stairs.

He'd ordered it about a month ago. 28 days for delivery it said and it was spot on. He'd been a member of the Sherlock Holmes Society of Europe for sixteen years, and every few months, they sent out the catalogue of all the latest books on Holmes, and that month's selection along with details of the latest films to be made about him and the tours on which you could go with fellow enthusiasts to see the spots featured in each of the books. The book that came this month was entitled *Sherlock Holmes and the American Myth*. He'd read a review of it already. It was about how the Yanks believed that Holmes really did exist and that all efforts to convince them otherwise were fruitless.

'What is it?' Mother asked.

'Some old *Reader's Digest* stuff. It still comes even though I asked them to stop,' he told her.

'It's them English, isn't it? They'll keep ramming that stuff down your throat. They're still at it trying to make us like them,' she said, before putting another three spoons of sugar into her tea and buttering more bread for herself. He sat down and poured himself some more tea and looked out at the blue skies outside.

God, how he hated these sunny mornings. It was early October, the feckin' sun should be gone for the year now. When it shone in through the windows above the door, it lit up the hallway like some sort of antiquated Newgrange. It made him feel like he should be outside doing some job or helping on the boats or cleaning up the sheds. No, he preferred the rain because that way there was a genuine reason for being indoors and reading or writing letters to these societies who knew him only by his notes and would not pass any sort of judgment on him. He had a letter from a professor ten years ago in Alberta as a result of a letter he wrote to the *Holmes Journal*. And it was on a specially

Nightmusic

embossed writing paper from the university over there where the professor taught English. He was a Holmes fanatic as well and they corresponded regularly. Malachy only stopped writing when the professor said that he was coming to Ireland for a convention and he'd call in. Malachy didn't want that, so he discontinued the letters to Alberta in case some learned fucker turned up on the doorstep one day and where would ya put him? Probably a shirt-lifter anyway, Malachy thought, so there's no point encouraging them. Still, 'twas nice while it lasted, the chats with the educated man, the man of letters. Malachy had told the professor that he shared a birthdate with Mozart and the professor had sent over a copy of the film *Amadeus*, but it was on the wrong video format so Malachy could never watch it. However, he went down to the video store a few weeks later and got out the VHS version and watched it three times in one night, but it pissed him off a bit because he didn't like the Mozart in that film. So he burnt it in the range to stop the video store renting it to anyone else. And never went back to explain.

He never tried explaining Sherlock Holmes to Mother. She'd never understand the fascination he had with the creation. He'd sat down with her once and watched Basil Rathbone in the *The Hound of the Baskervilles* but she left for bed halfway through it, saying it was rubbish. He wanted to throw something at her that night, but she'd disappeared around the corner of the stairs before he'd found anything suitable, so he put the log down again and continued watching the film. It was great, better than the book. He had the entire collection now and different editions of some of them. He had some great books about Bernard Spilsbury as well. Spilsbury was one of the finest pathologists Britain had ever produced and there were lots of books about him, even some with pictures. Pictures of bodies. And stories about Dr. Crippen and some other great killers.

He noticed how her limp wasn't as bad as it used to be now. It had been over a year since she had fallen over the cat, and in the meantime she had been very quiet, not doing anything to annoy him at all. If she kept it up like that, she might never fall over the cat again. As for the falls she'd already had, well, she deserved those. They were coming for a long time. When she threw those books of his into the range; when she hid his watch; when she locked the shutters hard on the window so that not even a smidgeen of light would get through when he was a child and frightened of the dark. Those were the reasons she had to fall over the cat from time to time. Even if she was old and frail, people should think of these things when they're doing them so that they won't have to pay later. Isn't that what religion is all about? Live a good life now so that you can benefit later. That's what you're told, but this was his Heaven and he was God.

After breakfast, he placed the dishes in the sink, washed them, left them on the draining board and went up to his room and unwrapped the package again, taking out the book, but he left that to one side, preferring instead to read the brochure offering weeks away with other Sherlock Holmes fans. He read with interest the itinerary of each trip, but he knew that no matter how much he read about Holmes, he could never bring himself to converse openly about him with strangers. Most of those others are probably the likes of those who were at that first Mozart concert he'd attended back in the college more than twenty five years beforehand. You wouldn't be able to talk to them, with their heads up their holes. Anyway, these trips cost a lot of money. Still, there probably wasn't much he could learn on one of those trips that he didn't already know. However, he didn't throw it out, and placed it carefully into the bottom of the drawer beside his bed.

* * * *

Nightmusic

Fogarty could hear them before he saw them, and perhaps could even smell them as well. There were four or five of the usual crew sitting at the back of the carpark just off Eyre Square, each holding a bottle and each conducting a surprisingly articulate conversation with at least one of the others. They had found a little alcove in the old church where they could snuggle in out of the rain and away from the prying eyes of the passers-by, like in the Square where tourists were now taking their pictures, can ya believe that? And nuns. They got a lot of nuns asking them where it had all gone wrong. They had lost count of how many nuns they had told to fuck off. But here, they were assured of a little peace and quiet, especially now after hours when the car park was closed and the security guards wouldn't be around hassling them.

They got a start when they saw the uniform come around the corner towards them.

'Fuck, the shades, the shades,' said the ringleader Tony Loftus when they saw Fogarty coming and they got up to run.

'Stall where ye are.'

They stalled for the shade.

'Howya, guard. Are ya here to arrest me again? I done nothing the last time but ya still arrested me.'

'Aisy lads, that's an awful fuckin' hostile attitude to adopt to a member of the Garda Siochana,' said Fogarty. 'For a minute there I thought ye didn't like me or something. If I arrested ya, ya must have done something wrong and I'll do it again if you're not careful.'

They sat down again and continued to sup from the bottles, looking sheepish and upset that their hovel had been infiltrated.

'We're doing nothing here. When we were down Merchants Road we were moved on, and in the Square, and now here. Will ya ever lave us alone?'

'I'm not moving ye on. I've no problem with ye. I'm here about Bridie.'

'We didn't do anything to her.'

'I know that but I want to find out what did happen to her. She got an awful doing over with the train.'

'We heard about it.'

'Had she a bike?'

'She was a fuckin' bike more likes...' said another but Loftus turned on him. 'Don't spake ill of the dead like that, ya little bollocks. Bridie was often nice to yourself so she was and now you're ...'

'Sorry Tony, I was only joking, like. I didn't mean any of it. I was having the laugh like.'
'Well, a laugh is one thing, but at the expense of the dead, well, that's not fuckin' on, so it's not.'
Another one of them with a shaved head was saying nothing, and looked away every time Fogarty asked him a question or looked in his direction.
Fogarty went down on his hunkers.
'What I want to know is how she got out the railway line, nearly as far as Oranmore at half nine when she was sitting here drunk earlier that evening after the Mass next door.'
'We're saying nothing to the shades. They never did us any fuckin' favours,' said Loftus.
'Let ye have it that way then,' said Fogarty as he got up to go. 'But don't come crawling to us the rest of ye when the next one of ye is done. First Martin Kilkelly and now Bridie Maloney. There's some fucker out there taking ye all and doing ye in. Don't say ye weren't warned.'
'We don't need anyone to look out for us. It's not as if ya gave a shite about us or anything.'
'What do ya want me to do? Haul ye in and ask ye below in the station.'
They stopped drinking. And started chatting among themselves.
The little bald fella said something to Loftus as Fogarty walked away and he heard Loftus say, 'Tell him, so, if ya want to.'
He got up and came after him.'
'Guard.'
'What?' said Fogarty, looking at the fella hobbling towards him, for all the world the dead spit of the character Dustin Hoffman played in *Midnight Cowboy*.
'There is something, Guard.'
'Well, spit it out.'
'I was here the night she went missing ...'
'Right.'
'I was talking to her earlier, but I was having a slash over there when I saw her going.'
'And was she walking or what?'
'No, Guard, she didn't need a bike to go to Oranmore. She got a seat.'
'A seat. Who'd fuckin' give her a seat?'
''Dunno who he was, but he parked over there and spoke to her.'
'Did ya know him?'

'No, but she spoke to him back. Maybe he was riding her, Guard.'
'You're filling me with shite now, are ya?'
'No, Guard, I swear on me mother's grave. I was worrying about it since then, but Loftus didn't want us to say anything. He wanted us to find out for ourselves.'
'What did he want ye to find out for yerselves?'
He looked over his shoulder.
'Ever since Kilkelly went missing, he thinks that auld enemies are coming after us.'
'Auld enemies.'
'From years back, when we were in the gang up in Bohermore, like. He thought it might be the warriors.'
'Warriors.'
'The warriors. The knackers. Up from Tuam like. Ya know, the pavees.'
'And why did ya think it might be the knackers?'
''Twas parked over there, sir. The van. The van she got into. It looked like one of their vans. It was a green one.'
Fogarty moved closer.
'A green van. Are ya sure?'
'I am, guard, I am.'
'And who was the sham driving it?'
'Didn't get to see them proper like, Guard.'
'Sure that's no good to me, ya must have got a look at them.'
'But it couldn't have been the warriors though, really.'
'Why do ya say that?" asked Fogarty.
'Cos of the number, sir. 'Twas a Galway van, an eighty-nine one and, sure the warriors only ever have new vans.

* * * *

Nightmusic

The Chief was on the warpath when Morley got into the newsroom. It was a Tuesday morning and there was still no sign of the feature on the local elections that he was supposed to have written. The elections were happening the following year and the Chief was looking forward to buckets of cash from advertising.

Elections are a godsend for the local newspapers. As all political advertising is banned on local radio, the papers clean up as there is nowhere else for the parties to go. And with 30 county council seats in Galway and 15 in the city up for grabs, there'd be at least 100 candidates running and if you could get the guts of a grand's worth of advertising out of most of them, then you were laughing. And the Chief wanted to make sure the *Chronicle* got started early on its political coverage so the sales team could start working on the parties.

This article was supposed to be the one that kick started this.

And there was no sign of it.

He had told Morley the previous week that he wanted a 2,000 word article on who was likely to do well in the poll and he wanted it done on an electoral area by area basis. Basically, he wanted everyone's name in there and he didn't want anyone's chances to be rubbished in the article. Just yet. There was plenty of time for objective comment later. This was a sales drive. And Morley had broken his own golden rule by promising he'd have it done before it was finished.

He'd left the newsroom by the time Morley came in. The others in the newsroom put their heads down. They knew that Morley had forgotten all about it. They knew too that there was no point going into the Chief's office now and telling him that he didn't have it done because there was a page waiting to be filled with it and he wanted it this morning. Morley had intended to go around and talk to a few of the candidates, but in a situation like this he'd have to wing it, so he switched on his iMac and started typing away. 2,000 words could be written inside an hour if you were flowery enough, so he started, writing notes on each candidate as he went. 2000 words divided by 100 candidates meant little on each, but who cared? It was a matter of filling white space, and he hoped he'd have the guts of it knocked out by the time the Chief came back. But then the phone rang and he received the grand summons.

Morley went up and knocked on the door.

Nightmusic

'Ya wanted to see me, Chief?'
'No, not you. I wanted to see your bloody article. It just so happens that you were the one who was supposed to write it. Have you it ready?'
'I had it done. I did it on the laptop at home but I think the disc got corrupted.'
'Corrupted? Appropriate for the political piece. But can ya save it? What does corrupt mean? Is it fucked? Is that what you're saying, man?'
'I don't know sir, but I'll try and see what I can do. If not, I might have to write it out again.'
'Again. It's a fuckin' Tuesday, Morley. You should be working on front page news at this stage. Not on an inside page feature which you should have done already.'
'But I had it done...'
'If it was for the fuckin' English tabloids, you'd have it done, I'm sure.'
Morley didn't want the argument to go down that avenue as there was only one winner. The best thing is to put the head down and brave it out. The Chief would cool down.
'I can have it by lunchtime and I'll stay on late tonight for the front page stuff,' he said.
'All right. Get cracking,' said the Chief as he waved him away. There was no point hanging around for compliments or even politeness, so Morley got up and left and went back to his piece. He had asked the others to list out all the candidates for him before he went up to the Chief, so from there on, it was just a matter of bullshitting a little about them all. Community activist, popular party figure, behind the scenes worker, travellers rights candidate, anti dump candidates, anti roads candidates, anti incinerator candidate, anti and uncle candidates, they were all in there and when they saw their name in print in a pseudo-serious political piece for the first time, they'd be back for advertising. The creative juices were flowing, the hyperbole was acting the hyperbolics and the piece was taking shape. And then his mobile rang. The others looked up, always eager to listen in on his conversations with news editors from other papers looking for stuff in which he'd promise them the earth and play them off against each other. Everything was 'no bother. I'll see ya get this as soon as possible' and if the story was good enough, he'd flog it to all the papers before giving it back to those who originally commissioned him. But this wasn't the papers.
It was Fogarty. An out of breath Fogarty.
'I hope you're out searching for vans.'

'No, I'm in the office.'
'We're down to 43 vans. The van had an 89 reg so taking out the campers and Transits, there's light at the end of the tunnel. Can you come out and give me a hand this evening?'
'No, I'm up to me balls here doing work I should have done last week.'
'So ya can't help me, then?'
'No.'
'Some hard hack you are.'
'Every hard hack has to do the bread and butter stuff. Wolf from the door and all that.'
'There's no fuckin' wolf near your door. He's well down the garden path.'
'Huh.'
'I spoke to the winos at the church where Bridie Maloney was last seen. She got into a green van as well. And it had an 89 reg.'
'Are ya sure?'
Morley knew the others in the newsroom were listening, so he got up and went into the toilet with the phone, putting down the lid and sitting on the loo, well out of earshot.
'Well, I'm only going on what the witness saw, but I think he's telling the truth,' said Fogarty. 'We could be on to something. I'm going to the Super with this next week if I can tie it down.'
'OK, keep me informed will ya? Remember, I want to have the story. No point giving it to the Super if he's going to give it all to RTE or someone else. He goes soft at the sight of a camera. He likes getting his mug on RTE and fuck the local lads. Don't do anything without tellin' me. We had a deal, right?'
'Right.'
And then he hung up. Without a goodbye.

* * * *

Nightmusic

'Golf Alpha to Five-seven. Come in please.'
'Five-seven. Go-ahead,' said Fogarty, sitting back in the passenger seat of the squad car, squinting out at the punters walking up Salthill.
'Call coming in about a domestic in Knocknacarra, No. 6 Cinnamon Gardens.'
'Right. Over.'
'Came from a neighbour. Can you check it out?'
'Will do. Over and out.'
Catherine Kelly was driving the car, so she turned it at the roundabout at the Seapoint and headed back out along the Prom.
'Amazing, isn't it?' said Fogarty. 'These fuckers with the big houses in Knocknacarra, rowing like that. I remember once there was never a call from Knocknacarra. It was just the usual places and now there's one every bloody night out there.'
'Changing times, Noel. Too much money or too much overdraft.'
'Did ya know?' said Fogarty, 'they used to call Knocknacarra Hamburger Hill, because they all had such huge mortgages they could only afford hamburgers.'
'Really?'
'God's honest truth,' he said. 'A butcher told me that. When the place was built first, they all had massive mortgages and it seems ya had to have an Irish name to live there too. Place is full of them with strange long Irish names. They're a right bollocks to be writing down. Every house has them, and the kids as well, long strings of fadas and focails.'
'Maybe they get a grant for it. It's in the Gaeltacht, isn't it?'

Fogarty didn't like working the 10pm to 6am shift, because it meant that you had to get kip during the day and that's not possible in a house full of kids and with the light peeping through the curtains.
He told the kids once that whatever they did when they grew up, make sure they get a job that doesn't involve working nights. 'It ruins your lifes,' he told them, but they were too young to understand. Maybe they would some day.
To make it worse, he didn't even have that kip today because he was too busy checking out green vans. He'd gone through 36 of them and most of them were in a right mess and only a handful were still on the road. He'd made a few calls out the county again and eliminated a few more, so there were only five or six left to do the following day, but he'd have to get to bed first or he'd collapse. How could he sleep, though,

with the knowledge that his investigation could be all for nought if there was nothing to be found in the last few vans? Most of the ones he had left were in and around the city anyway, so the likelihood is that they might have some involvement.

When they got to the house in Knocknacarra, a man was outside roaring. but he quietened when he saw the squad car. He came to the window of the squad car and pointed at the upstairs bedroom window. 'Did she call ye out, the mad bitch? She's in there and she's locked me out of my own home.'
'Calm down,' said Fogarty, while Kelly went to the door and rang the bell. She could see people at windows around the estate, looking out at the sideshow. She knelt down and shouted through the letter box. 'Open the door. This is the Gardai. You're OK, just open the door so we can talk.'
No reply.
The man roared 'Bitch,' but Fogarty told him that if he did that again, he'd arrest him for a breach of the peace.
But as Fogarty was walking towards the door of the house, there was an almighty crash upstairs as the bedroom window smashed and a portable TV came through, landing on the lawn just feet from the man who was staggering around the grass. It smashed into bits and was followed by videotapes.
The woman came to the window.
'Here, take your TV and dirty videos. Show these to your friends in the Gardai then.'
'I didn't ring them. You rang them, you stupid bitch.'
'I didn't. You pulled out the phone, remember.'
'Oh yes, I forgot. Oops. You had to start roaring, didn't you?'
Fogarty asked the woman to open the door again, but she told him to 'Fuck off and go and catch some real criminals.' At that he ran at the front door and gave it an almighty kick. It crashed in before him. With Kelly behind him, he ran up the stairs and into the front room where the woman was throwing a small video recorder out the window. He caught her just as it went through another pane and crashed on the lawn below. He could see the man outside with the smashed TV, throwing it at a Ford Ka parked in the drive and shouting, 'You break my stuff, I'll break yours,' and he sent the TV remnants in through the side window of the car. Kelly caught the woman as she grappled with

Nightmusic

Fogarty and threw her onto the bed, restraining her from behind, before cautioning her for causing a breach of the peace.

Then Fogarty went downstairs and arrested the man on a similar charge.

'I know Superintendent Quigley and he'll have you transferred to Tory Island.'

Fogarty looked around, lifted his leg and gave the man a kick up the hole.

'Transfer this, will ya, while you're at it?' The man was shocked, he probably hadn't been kicked in the arse for thirty years. Kelly came down and put the woman in beside him in the back seat. They handcuffed them and brought them back to the station.

Fogarty had a cut on his face, probably from the flying glass from the bedroom window, and Kelly put some disinfectant on it for him and it stung.

'Like the *War of the Roses*, wasn't it?' she said, but Fogarty didn't know what she meant.

'The film, with Danny de Vito and Kathleen Turner. The couple fighting. It was like that.'

'Haven't seen that one. But they're mad fuckers, they deserved each other.'

When he got home, he put on a breakfast for himself, and the kids, who were just getting up. He couldn't believe how early kids got up nowadays. When he was a kid, he'd stay in bed until nine o clock and make a quick dash to the school. But now they were up and ready at ungodly hours, like 6.30 a.m.

He made a saucepan of porridge. The kids used to hate it but then they saw some cartoon called *The Magic Porridge* and ever since then they loved it, when he got a chance to make it. He shouldn't have had the energy to do it, but he was on a high after the night, and knew he wouldn't get any rest until they were picked up for school and the house was quiet again.

They came down and started packing the lunchboxes, but he emptied them again and did it properly.

Then Mary came down, wearing a dressing gown, but looking like he felt, with her hair tied back neatly with a lovely brown clip. She opened the lunchboxes and prepared them even more properly.

Fogarty looked at her without saying anything as he stirred the porridge. That was the thing about her. No matter how well you could do something, she could do it better. There was no limit to her general talents. Or common sense. She always had a solution.

'Busy night.'
'Yeah. Raid on the Headford Road and the mother of all rows out in Knocknacarra. TVs and videos flying.'
'Male, female, domestic. The usual I suppose.'
'Yeah, nail on the head, luv.'
'Are ya going up for a while?' she said to him looking at him in a pitying sort of way. His hair was standing on his head and his eyes were bloodshot.
'Yeah, after I eat something.'
'Might join ya.'
'No classes today, or what?'
'Mine are out on work experience. Just have to make a few phonecalls, but that can wait until later.'
'Oh, am I on a promise?'
'Play your cards right,' she said, biting on a slice of toast.
'I have to get up in the afternoon, though. Few things to check out.'
'Work, is it?'
'Yeah, sort of.'

He looked around the kitchen at his smiling daughters, his sexy wife and the nice smells coming from the saucepan of the warm oatmeal. Life could be beautiful sometimes. The sun could shine on the city and everything would look so great. Here he was. Man the hunter, in from the wilds and his womenfolk around him as he cooked the oatmeal. He felt like Papa Bear with a house full of Goldilocks, all waiting for their porridge.
But the kids didn't like it this morning.
It was tough and lumpy and burned their tongues a bit.
So they had toast instead.

* * * *

Nightmusic

Fogarty liked Shantalla. And Mervue and Bohermore and some parts of Newcastle, as they were real Galway. Ordinary houses with ordinary people. No townhouses and apartments. No students. No four-wheel drives driven by the recently wealthy. Just ordinary folk. Salt of the earth. The type you could knock on their doors and they'd come out and help ya. But the new Galway was creeping in fast. On the edge of all of these areas, the townhouse mentality was setting in and soon all these little houses might be gone for ever. A few houses had disappeared down near the corner.

He'd been in a lot of those areas this morning checking out vans, mainly belonging to mechanics and builders, and now he was down to just two or three.

Even though he'd called Malachy Lee many's the time to come and get a body out of the river, he'd never looked to see what kind of van he had. He should have known that. He'd know less, he told himself. Nice fella, Malachy. Very obliging. Very sound. Not a glory seeker at all. Not in it for the money. Not like those snotty feckers with the bigger boats who'd never give ya a hand after dark on the river. No sipping wine at the Oyster festival for Malachy.

He knew by the absence of the van that Malachy wasn't there, but Mrs. Lee might know where he was. He reached into his pocket and switched off his mobile phone, then knocked at the door and held his breath to see if there was any noise coming from inside the house, but there wasn't.

He knocked again and still there was no reply, so he went down the path at the side of the house, to the gate that led into the back garden. An old woman sat on a chair on a concrete area outside the back door. She was playing with a cat, stroking its neck so that it came back and rubbed against her harder and harder like cats do, the selfish bastards.

'Hello.'

She looked up.

'Hello, sorry for coming around the back like this. Is Malachy here?'

'Who are ya?'

'Oh, I'm a friend of his. Noel Fogarty is the name. I'm a guard in town. I know him from the jobs he does for us.'

'What did ya say yer name was again?'

'Noel Fogarty.'

Nightmusic

'Fogarty. I never heard him say anything about ya. Are ya anything to the Fogartys in Doughiska?'
'No, ma'am. I'm not from town at all.'
'Malachy mentioned the superintendent, though. D'ya know him?'
'Yeah, I know him, ma'am.'
'He's nice to Malachy.'
'Yah, he would be.'
'What do ya want him for? Is there someone else in the water?'
'No, just a few bits and bobs I wanted to ask him. He's gone, is he? The van isn't there.'
'No, he went off a while ago. He's very busy now. What with the docks and the farm. He has his own farm.'
'Where?'
'It was my brother's place out past Furbo. I never thought he'd like it, but he goes there a lot. Even though to be honest I never see the work he's doing, but it's that kind of place. Overgrown with weeds and nettles and rusted sheds. He'd need to win the Lotto to do it up.'
'Does he have cattle or sheep, ma'am?'
'No, not at all. Sure where would he get the time for that? Will ya have tea?'
'No ma'am, I'm just after, ya know ... I'm grand now.'
It had often struck Fogarty that if there was anything Malachy Lee had plenty of, it was time. He was always available to come to help if he was called out. And as for work on the docks, Malachy had done damn all there for years. He signed on every week, he knew that because he'd seen him when he was watching some other fella some time back.
'He's a great lad, Mrs. Lee. Ya must be very proud of him.'
'Aye, he's good alright. He looks after me well. I don't be great on the walk, ya see. He's able to carry me. Up the stairs, like.'
'Is that your cat?'
'Well, he comes around a bit. I hadn't seen him for ages. I fell over him a few times or maybe it wasn't this one exactly, but a cat's a cat. So Malachy tries to keep him out of the house, but he's nice isn't he?'
'He is,' said Fogarty, leaning over and tickling the cat behind the ear.
'Malachy's a great help to us.'
'Aye, he does be telling me about the poor unfortunates in the water. That student from Mayo, the fella who killed himself.'
'Yes.'
'Shockin' that was. Shockin' and the girleen from Newcastle.'

Nightmusic

It's a terrible city, Mrs. Lee, there's a lot of pain out there.'
'And then there was the girl who was drowned in Dangan. The one the fisherman caught at the Salmon Weir. He tells me about them all.'
'Aye.'
Hang on, thought Fogarty. Jessica Kelly didn't go in in Dangan. At least, nobody ever said she did. But, it would make sense if she ended up in the Salmon Weir if she had, but how would she ever get to there from the Prom? How had she worked that one out in her confused mind? What was Malachy telling his mother?
'I was off myself that night. The night the girl went in at Dangan. Was Malachy there himself for that?' asked Fogarty.
'I don't know. He wasn't here anyway because that was the night of the Assumption and we used to go to Knock for a lot of years, but it's too much for me now, so we said the Rosary here and then he went out to go for a drink in the Westpark. He was there with the lads from the boat because he was saying that Martin Kennedy was asking for me. That's Nora's nephew. Nora Kennedy. She was a friend of mine for years and she helped me deliver Malachy. He's working in there, manager or something, and he was asking for me, so he was. And that was the night because he was all spruced up before the Rosary. He had a bath and all. I thought he might be meeting a girl, but no fear of that. He likes his independence too much.'
'Maybe he's better off, Mrs. Lee, maybe he's better off.'
'Arragh, I don't know. It might settle him a bit, instead of all that nonsense of books and foreign music, depressing aul' stuff he plays up in his room.'
'Sure, listen, Mrs. Lee, I'd better be getting off. Sure I'll give him a ring later on. It's not that important anyway. Goodbye now.'
'Goodbye. And Guard?'
'Yes, Mrs. Lee?'
'Ya forgot to say goodbye to the cat.'
Fogarty fired a farewell to the feline, waved and went around the corner.

* * * *

The *Chronicle* was out, so Morley could take a half-day. His election piece adorned page three and looked very well with a few pictures and a drawing of a ballot box. It was written in about two and a half hours and all of the candidates loved it because it was nice to them all. The Chief was delighted too because he'd already had a phone call from the directors of elections for the two main parties. They told him they wanted six weeks of quarter pages and four halves and if necessary could he keep a few full pages for them, depending on how the budget was stretching. The Chief thought the article was interesting and he'd have loved to tell Morley so, but it was not in his nature. No point showing them he was getting soft in his old age.

Morley rang the station to see if Fogarty was on duty that day but was told that he wasn't due on until 10 that night. But he wasn't answering his mobile and he told him never to ring the house because they'd be able to see if any calls were incoming or outgoing if the whole thing went pear shaped. He kept dialling, but still all he got was "the customer you are calling may be out of range or have their unit powered off" message. He couldn't even leave a message, so thinking of Fogarty's advice about the fast food, he went to the gym and ran for 45 minutes on a treadmill to try to burn off the effects.

* * * *

The Westpark was a real hards' pub. It was like the sort of thing you'd find on the Shankill Road, but it was here in Galway and even more unShankilly, was full of small moustachioed Celtic-jersey wearing soccer fans, roaring on their team on the big screen to some facile victory against Motherwell. Fogarty had his grey fleece on over his shirt as he moved through the crowd towards the bar.
'What can I get ya?'
'Is Martin Kennedy here?'
'He's down the back. Through the door there.'
The place erupted as Larsson broke through and hit a shot which came back off a post. Three hundred and fifty people with three hundred and fifty different coloured moustaches said 'fuck' in three-hundred and fifty different dialects. He made his way down the side of the bar to the toilets and to the door marked Private.
He knocked and went through. Inside there was a man with a cup of coffee sending a text message on his phone. He looked up when Fogarty came in.
'Sorry the jacks is out there. It's staff only in here.'

Nightmusic

"Martin Kennedy?'
'Yeah.'
'Noel Fogarty, Garda Noel Fogarty.'
Kennedy sat up and put down the phone.
'Just checking something out. Do ya know Malachy Lee from Shantalla?'
'I know him, yeah. His mother is a friend of me aunt.'
'When did ya see him last?'
'Jaysus. Maybe school. Why?'
'Did you meet him in here on August 15th and tell him yer aunt was asking for his mother?'
'Did I fuck? I haven't seen Mal for about twenty years. No, I'm wrong. I saw him two years ago at the races. He was all done up with a suit on him and a pair of binoculars, but I didn't talk to him. He's a weird fucker.'
'You're sure about this?' asked Fogarty.
'That he's a weird fucker? Yeah, I am.'
'No, are ya sure ya haven't seen him since?'
'Yeah. Why? Did he do something wrong?'
'No, it's just routine. Trying to eliminate people from an enquiry, ya know how it is.'
'Oh right.'
He made his way out through the bar where it was now considerably quieter. Celtic had gone a goal down and Martin O'Neill was lepping around the sideline like a man demented.

Fogarty got into his car and rang Morley's mobile, but it just rang and rang without answer. And why would it be answered, stuck down where it was in between towels and shorts and sweaty socks in his gym bag in the locker. Third time he rang it, he let it go onto the answering machine.
'Give me a ring when ya get this message. I'll be on the mobile. I'm going to meet someone, so I'll talk to ya later.'
He smiled to himself and put his mobile back into his pocket.

* * * *

Nightmusic

The dinner plate crashed onto the ground, scattering potatoes all over the floor. Malachy followed it with a glass which smashed on the side of the sink. Then he brought his fists down on the table with such force, it made her cry.

He looked at his hands and they were shaking now. He'd nearly thrown up when she told him that she'd had a visitor.

'Have you no sense, Mother? How many times have I told you? How many?'

'Lots. Lots, Malachy,' she sobbed.

'Then why did you let him stay? Ya should have ran him.'

'But he seemed such a nice man. He knew you. Said he was a guard.'

'It doesn't matter. That's how they get into your confidence. Was he in the house?'

'No, he was just in the garden looking for you. He didn't ask for money or anything?'

'How do you know he didn't have an accomplice?'

That's what Holmes would have done. He'd have made Watson divert attention and then go in himself and check something out.

He thumped the table again.

'I'm sorry about this Mother, but I just get so angry. Stop crying.'

She continued to sob.

'I get this way because I care for you and I don't want you being attacked by muggers or confidence tricksters getting into the house. I told you and told you and told you and still you let a strange man into the back garden and probably into the house too if he wanted to. You always said keep to ourselves and let our business be our business. But if you're going to let people into the house, then it's not ours anymore and for Christ's sake, stop crying.'

He got up and started clearing up the potatoes. 'Eat up. Eat yours, I'll get something for myself here.'

He picked up the potatoes and then went over to the sink and started gathering the shards of glass. He took a plastic bag from the press and put the potatoes and glass into it and then threw it into the bin.

'You have a fierce temper. Like yer father,' she said.

But he said nothing, just took one look back as he went around the corner of the stairs, and saw that Mother was still sobbing, her grey head shaking back and forth, the stupid old cow.

He went up to his room, but nothing had been touched. They hadn't

Nightmusic

gotten in here anyway. Who's to say there weren't three or four of them and that one had distracted Mother while she was out the back. They operate like that, undercover and sneaky, breaking into people's homes and searching them and tapping their phones and putting bugs in the rooms and maybe small cameras. No, they had infiltrated his home now so it would never be as safe again. It was time to change the commonplace.

Watson, if criminals would always schedule their movements like railway trains, it certainly would be more convenient for all of us.

He bundled his Sherlock Holmes brochures and grabbed the emergency bag which contained everything he'd need to get away in a hurry. He'd packed it seven years ago in the knowledge that there would be a time like this when he would need it. He opened it every six months to replace the toothpaste and the perishables and to add some more money from his account and to update the clothes. Now, the money was all in £50 notes, wrapped in bundles tightly bound with elastic bands. He had about 40 of them forming a layer at the bottom of the bag. He'd saved one for every month since he started having guests at the cellar. Sometimes, he took the money from them, but mostly, it was saved from the odd jobs at the docks and on the boats, when he'd go out off Inishbofin with the lads from the Claddagh. He'd cut a sleeve inside the bag where he placed the new passport he got two years before, even though he'd never used the first one. He took out his list and went through it, line by line, item by item. Things to include, things to get rid of. He stayed in there for two hours and listened when Mother made her own way up the stairs, hobbling along around the bend and into the toilet. He heard her sit inside for a few minutes and then flush the loo and wash her hands. He waited until she came out and made her way across the landing. Then he switched off the light, went behind her and roaring 'Mind that fucking cat, Mother,' he placed his arms in the small of her back and pushed and shut his eyes until he heard the thumps and the moans and then the silence. Then he stepped over her slumped body on the stairs, and with his bags in his arms, went out the door.

* * * *

Nightmusic

The dog next door woke up in a hurry as the van revved up and drove away around the corner and down towards Cooke's Corner and through the lights as they went amber before red. It was that trangression that caught Fogarty's eye. He'd been waiting at the bottom of the hill for Malachy to come back and leave again, but even he was taken aback by the speed of his sudden departure. He followed the van, about three cars behind, hoping the lights would favour him at Lower Salthill which they did. And they did again in the resort itself before heading onto the Prom. Two of the cars ahead of Fogarty had turned in different directions so there was just one car between his and the van, so he allowed another to come out as they all moved at an easy pace along the prom, past Leisureland and the Galway Bay Hotel, and out the coast road.

With his cover varying, he held well back about four hundred yards behind the van, but he didn't want Malachy to get too far ahead. However, he remembered that Mrs. Lee had said the farm was out past Furbo, so he'd be on the main road for a while anyway.

Just after Furbo, the van disappeared to the right and the other cars carried out straight heading towards Spiddal. With nothing between himself and the van, he took his time taking the corner, and did so just as the van went out of sight at the next bend. However, when Fogarty went around that bend, he could see there was nowhere for his car to hide, as ahead lay a mile or two of winding open bog road, leading across to a cluster of trees and some outbuildings on the far side. He watched as Malachy's van continued out towards the far side. He pulled the car into the darkest part of the small wooded area and waited and watched. He leant over and searched in the dash for the small binoculars Mary had given him for going to the races, but he never wore them because he was never off for the races anyway with all leave cancelled. He took them out of their leather case and unfolded them, adjusting the lens until he could see the tail-lights of the van go into the trees and stop. There was a sharp bleep bleep from his mobile and he picked it up, but it was only the battery warning. He looked in the dash to see if the in-car charger was there. Fuck. It wasn't. Why the fuck had he brought the in-car charger out of the car and into the house? But he had. Fucking eejit. After about fifteen minutes, he saw the van turning and coming back across the bog, its lights just barely on as it ambled along. Parked behind the trees, Fogarty's car was well concealed as the van made its way out the boreen, past the trees, down into the village and back onto the main road. Fogarty waited before starting the ignition and driving slowly across the bog, each crunch of the wheels on the gravel sending a shiver up his spine until he was close to the farmyard, its buildings rundown and dark, and its appearance untidy and uncared for. Whatever Malachy was doing here, it certainly wasn't maintenance. This place was sure to be haunted, he thought to himself, He reached over and took out the torch and opened the doors. This would have been a nice farm once, he thought, but now it just looked neglected and spooky. With the light fading, every window was like a socket in a skull, every breeze through the trees a wailing banshee. He went over to the house, and pushed in the door, but the roof had fallen in and a dark pile of rotten thatch and timber lay in the centre of what would once have been a living room. The rooms off that were full of old furniture and contained two broken High Nelly bicycles and loads of fertiliser bags. He went across to the small outhouses, but they were wet and muddy and covered in large cobwebs, which stuck to his face as he went through. At the back of these buildings was the barn, which was the only place to be secured. Its red gate was rusting, but Fogarty went back to the car and took out the crowbar from the boot, and wrenched the door out on one side until the gap was large enough for him to squeeze through, snagging his fleece as he did so.

Inside, the floor was clear and there was an old cart which hadn't been used for years. He pointed the torch around the walls, lighting up shelves of tins of paint and old tools and a scythe and several spades. The floor was covered with leaves and twigs but in one section, these had been brushed aside to reveal a bolted rectangular door in the floor in the corner. He bent down and grabbing hold of the bolt, pulled it back and lifted up one of the doors to reveal a cellar. Lifting back the second door, his light illuminated the timber steps down into a dark chamber. He stuck his head down and shone the light around what seemed like a large space. On one side, there was a switch held onto a wooden plank with a nail, so he turned it on and a lower room lit up as a fluorescent tube flickered into life, exposing a big area dominated by a large concrete table. He came down the steps and took a look at the room.
The wind howled through the small windows in the barn as he searched further, his torchlight still probing the shelves despite the fluorescent tubes overhead. There were boxes of condoms, some porn magazines,

Nightmusic

several half empty whiskey bottles, a roll of tape and several large brown medicine bottles. On the shelf below, there lay three instamatic cameras of varying age and model. Five or six rolls of broad insulating tape lay on the shelf below that and a scissors, some batteries and a large container of disinfectant.

On the next shelf there was a small silver stereo with a tape deck and a CD player. Morley pushed down the CD lid and it flipped up, revealing a CD of the Overture from *Don Giovanni* by Mozart, performed by the Royal Philharmonic. Other Mozart CD boxes lay stacked beside it and a bottle of liquid for cleaning discs.

But in behind the shelves, something was shining. He put his hand up and felt a sort of curtain covering a hole in the wall. He shone the light in and saw two small silver cases. He took one out. It was locked but taking a chisel from one of the toolboxes he forced it open. Inside, there were several packages, so he took one out. It was packed with photographs all wrapped with cling film and all showing the naked bodies of girls. They were amateurish blurred shots, some of the same ones taken over and over again, but not showing any faces. Just showing breasts, navels and pubic areas but never any faces. They were taken in different positions, but concentrated mainly on those areas. Fogarty thought he recognised something in them. He looked up from them and then at them again and then up again. Yes, it was the concrete table. The girls in the photos had all been lying on that. You could match the rough edges of it with those shown in the photos. He picked up another bundle and another and saw they were arranged into months and years. There were bundles here marked 1996. He reached in and got the second box and using the chisel again, he smashed the lock, revealing more bundles of photos. He searched frantically to see if any of the faces of the females were shown, but they weren't. He could see though that in many cases, their hands and legs were bound and there was blood on the table, huge streaks of it. In another bundle, there were photographs of underwear, neatly laid out on the floor.

He put his hand in his pocket and took out his mobile phone but it only had one bar of reception showing, so he decided to go above ground and outside to the yard where the signal would be better. He wondered should he ring Quigley first or just the officers to get a car out here. He made his way toward the steps and with his torch in one hand and his phone in the other, he climbed carefully, his head leaving the light and

Nightmusic

into the darkness above. In the darkness, he could make out the gap in the door where he had come through. He reached for it and then everything went dark, really dark and he fell to the floor.

* * * *

And when that darkness became light again, he felt his chest heaving and every breath was shorter than the last. Above him was the fluorescent tube, but when he moved to push himself up, he found he couldn't. Something trickled into his eye and stung him but he couldn't move his hands to wipe it clear, so he groaned loudly. He tried to move his head to one side, but that too was difficult. He flapped an eyelid quickly in a bid to take the fluid from his eye, but it was caked with it and now it ran down the outside of his nose. It was blood.

He pushed himself upwards and managed to get a better look around the room. He could get the strong smell of petrol and then someone came in.

'Ya just couldn't keep out of it, could ya? Ya had to poke yer nose into it. Typical guard.'

'Malachy, what the fuck are ya doing? Help me here. Help me up. I'm bleeding.'

Malachy went over and flicked through the CDs, took one from its case, blew at it, took the one out of the machine and pushed the new one down into place, before clicking the button and filling the room with *Eine Kleine Nachtmusik*.

'Do ya like Mozart? I'm playing this one for ya because it's one of his best known and it's better to ease ya in. No point wasting some of the good stuff on a guard.'

'Help me, Malachy. For fuck's sake.'

'It's called *Eine Kleine Nachtmusik*. That means A Little Nightmusic. So it's kinda appropriate, isn't it? It suits the mood a bit. Upbeat, yet mournful in places. Would ya say?'

'Malachy stop the fuckin' messin'. Let me out. You could be in enough trouble as it is without making it worse.'

'Trouble? Is it trouble you're talking about? I've been living in Galway 44 years and I've never been in trouble. The guards have never called to my house once to give out about me. I've been too good. There are others up the road and the guards are calling all the time, but I've never been in trouble. Not once. So what can happen to me now?'

'Malachy, cop on. What the fuck have ya done to me?'

'I know what you've seen and frankly that's too much for me. I'm sorry, Garda Fogarty. That's all I ever knew you as so don't call me Malachy. I'm Mr. Lee to you.'

'How did ya get in to this shite? This is very wrong. You need help, ya know.'

'Help. Sure we all need help in some way. I'm sure you're a bit messed up as well.'
'This is very wrong, Malachy. You won't get away with this. The guards are on their way.'
'No, they're not. I checked your phone and the last call was to someone else.'
'Ah, for fuck's sake, Malachy, cut the ties on me.'
'You are powerless, Guard, so ask me any questions. You're going to die. Ya have to. Let there be no doubt about that, so let me be your last interrogation. I always wondered what I'd say when I had someone to talk to about all this.'
Fogarty shivered and tried to move but he was well secured. Now he had swallowed some of the blood and he felt like coughing but he could not lift himself high enough. Maybe it was better to humour Malachy. He spat out some blood but it landed back on his face.
'You're sick, Malachy. You must know you're sick because normally you're a reasonable man. You took people here and killed them, didn't you?'
'Maybe. You're getting warm.'
'You killed the girls this summer.'
'And last and the summer before that. You don't know what you have here. You'd become a bloody Commissioner if you could turn me in. But now you won't. Jeffrey and Dennis would be proud of me.'
'Who the fuck are Jeffrey and Dennis? Other sickos?'
'Oh, you don't know your crime do you? I suppose being a Garda in Galway is a world away from Dahmer and Nielsen.'
'Malachy, think about your mother, what she'd think if she knew you were here hurting young girls.'
'Not them all. I didn't kill them all.'
'What?'
'I didn't kill them all. Some of them were drugged in town, brought here, fucked and left back in town again. They never knew. It's just that some of them woke up on the way back. Tough luck on them.'
'That's sick.'
'What's sick about it? They went out on the town and were going to get screwed anyway, so why not by somebody who really appreciated it. It's happening all the time. It's just your crowd have no idea of how to stop it.'
'You bastard.'

Nightmusic

'Call me what you like, Guard. You're good at that, name-calling and throwing yer weight around, aren't ye?'

'Malachy, let's talk about this. I've never done anything on ya, tell me man to man why you're doing this? It's not right.'

'Man to man? Huh. This is the fastest growing city in Europe, Guard, and there is lots of money and lots of thrills. It's the kind of place you can get lost in for a while and then reappear, ya see. The city is full of drifters. They come to Galway, they take their chances and some meet me and some don't. It's kinda Russian roulette.'

'How d'ya mean?' Fogarty tugged at his arms again but they were well bound.

'It's not fair. Some people get everything or build something. Of their lives. But mine was gone since before I could change things. There are lots of little people in Galway too. People who've been walked on and who would love to be what all these blow-ins are.'

'That's shite, Malachy. You're as important as the next...'

'That's where you're wrong. The city is making money on the back of people like me who'll do all the shite jobs. I just want to be different. Not me. I hate being me. Look at me.'

'Listen, Malachy, I can help ya. Seriously I can. I'm a straight bloke. I've a family and I don't like being me often either. We've a lot in common.'

Malachy stood up and started slapping himself around the head.

'Concentrate, concentrate. Don't let them mess with you, Watson. Watson, don't let them in.'

Fogarty looked around and said, 'Who's Watson?' but Malachy just looked at him with disgust and continued slapping his own head.

The CD went onto the next track and Malachy went over and turned up the volume a bit.

'Listen to this one, Garda. It's *Mass in C Minor, Kyrie*. It's over eight minutes long. You should relax and enjoy it. That's what Mozart intended this piece for. Sort of ceremonial. And there you are on the slab and all. You should be privileged.'

'Sick fucker.'

'Now, now, don't be so crude. The town is full of people like me. I'm fed up of outsiders coming in and telling us what a great place we all live in because it serves bottles of beer by the neck and has 500-seater pubs. Now, it's time to take something back.'

'And murder and rape is the way, is it? That'll do the job all right, won't

Nightmusic

it?'

'Yes, it's very Stanley Kubrick, isn't it? Oh, you wouldn't know who he is. But it has that unreal feeling about it, would you say?'

He gathered up the photos and put them back into the cases.

'Time flies when you're enjoying yourself and I'm not going to hang around waiting for the cavalry. And neither are you. Enjoy the music,' he said as he disappeared up the ladder into the darkness. Fogarty could hear him moving around, dragging things and then he heard the gates open.

He looked over at the CD, the illuminated front said that the CD had played 7 minutes 48 seconds, but lifting his head was an effort so he let it fall back again. When he looked up again, Malachy was coming at him with a cloth in his hand and forcing it down onto his nose.

Watson, might I trouble you to open the window, for chloroform vapour does not help the palate.

* * * *

Nightmusic

Malachy stopped and stretched his arms at the shore. He had dragged Fogarty up that stairs and into the van. Now he had just laid him on the floor of the boat alongside the fishing rods and feathers and his arms were throbbing. Heavy bastard, that guard.

It was another quiet night on the bay with only a bit of a wave. The only lights were across in Ballyvaughan. Way out past the mouth of the bay, he could see a boat, probably a vessel heading from Doolin to Inis Oirr. He put the outboard onto the low gear and it purred out into the water, with Fogarty still prone on the floor. About a mile out, Malachy stopped the engine and leaned over the seat to grab Fogarty by the shoulders. He ripped the tape off his mouth and then off his legs and shook him to see if he was still unconscious, but there was no sign of movement out of him. It was awkward to pull a big man like Fogarty to the side of the boat without tipping it, so Malachy stood with his feet wide apart, and a boot on each side. He lowered his knife and slashed the tapes on Fogarty's arms and pulled away the tape. Then with his hands gripping Fogarty's fleece, he dragged him forward, threw one leg over the side and then the other, but as he did there was a loud splash as the Garda grabbed the side of the boat and lunged up at Malachy, his face locking in to the side of his head, and his teeth gnawing into his ear.

Malachy yelled and tried to grab the scissors to fight back, but as he did the boat wobbled from side to side and then capsized. He came up again and grabbed onto it and tried to right it, but Fogarty came at him again, punching him in the stomach and grabbing onto his leg. Malachy kicked and grappled onto the bottom of the upturned boat, but it was slippery and he could not hold it. Fogarty came at him again and Malachy pushed him underneath with a leg. Then Fogarty's head came up through the water and nutted Malachy in the balls, but as he did Malachy caught him between his knees under the water and closed his legs on the Garda's head. Fogarty punched at the legs again, to try and force them apart, but he was swallowing a lot of water. Once more Malachy felt himself slipping down the side of the boat, but he held the head between his legs and grabbed onto the ridge at the bottom of the boat and held on, holding the head and counting. The big Garda was still thrashing in the water as his arms flailed at Malachy's feet. Just 30 seconds more, Malachy told himself... 29, 28, 27, 26, 25, And that time went quickly and suddenly there was no more thrashing and no more bubbles but he held his legs closed all the same. He'd give him another minute just to make sure and even after that a bit more, but there wasn't much time for that as he was sinking too. The boat was now only just above the water and it would be difficult to right it. His arms were sliding off the side of the boat. He was tired and there was a dead man with his head stuck between his legs. He opened his knees and felt the weight of Fogarty slip away into the depths of Galway Bay, placing a foot on his shoulder to help him on his way.

The side of his face felt hot and oily and when he put his hand to his ear, he noticed some of it was gone. He wanted to feel it again to make sure, but every time he took his hand from the ridge of the boat, he slipped further into the water. Now he was marked, his perfect ear was damaged. Maybe he wouldn't be able to listen to Mozart anymore. Holmes didn't have any defects like that either. Now he was imperfect. Thoughts raced through his mind. He wondered if Mother had made her way up from the bottom of the stairs yet. He started to cry and tried once more to grab onto the side of the boat, but his grip was weak and slippery. He wanted to be back at home with the brochure and the books and the tape recorder. He wanted to come in and find the cocoa left in the mug and the kettle boiled for him. He'd dreamed of situations like this but then he always woke up safe. Now this was for real. He felt his legs cramp up and he gave one more push to try to get onto the upturned boat but his thighs felt heavy and he felt tired, and slowly, he just slid into the water.

* * * *

Nightmusic

Attn: Newsdesk
From: David Morley (Galway)

GARDA AND FISHERMAN MISSING AFTER FISHING ACCIDENT
Double tragedy for Galway fisherman's family

One man was drowned and another is missing after an accident on Galway Bay in the early hours of yesterday morning when the boat from which they were fishing capsized less than a mile from the shore. The two men, a Garda stationed in Galway city and a local fisherman, were reportedly out fishing for cod at the time of the accident.
The body recovered is that of Garda Noel Fogarty from Mill St., station in the city, while the man still missing is fisherman Malachy Lee from Shantalla.
Shocked neighbours and friends are also reeling from the news that Mr. Lee's elderly mother died early yesterday after she apparently fell down the stairs of the terraced home she shared with her son, possibly when she tried to raise the alarm that her son had not come home from fishing.
Gardai in Galway say there is no connection between the incidents and believe Delia Lee (71) stumbled and fell down the stairs in the house. Her body was found by neighbours at the house in Shantalla on the west side of Galway city.
Garda Fogarty was a past winner of a Scott Medal for bravery and a citation of honour from Galway Corporation for his efforts in rescuing people from perilous situations.
Mr. Lee was also well known in Galway city having helped out Gardai and lifeboat officials in many dangerous water rescues over the past few years.
Gardai in the city received a call from a witness who reported seeing the two men in difficulties and raised the alarm, scrambling the Sikorsky helicopter and the Galway Lifeboat, and at teatime yesterday, the body of Garda Fogarty was found near Black Rock at Salthill.
Further searches of the Bay continued throughout last evening for Mr. Lee but all that was found was more debris from the boat.
This is the first boating tragedy to hit the Bay for over ten years and locals are mystified as to why the two men ventured out at such a late hour.
However, Mr Lee is believed to have regularly taken fishing trips onto

Nightmusic

the Bay at night.
There was speculation that their outboard engine may have failed and that the men may have attempted to row ashore and subsequently capsized their boat.
The bodies of Garda Fogarty and Mrs. Lee were brought to Galway's University College Hospital where postmortems were being carried out late last night.
ends
(More details to follow as soon as soon as anything breaks) - DM

Morley typed the copy and spell checked it, before e-mailing it off to the nationals. Later, he rang the station for a quote from SuperQuigley who said that Fogarty had been an exemplary officer whose death was a blow to the force locally. He said Fogarty was an accomplished policeman who had on several occasions risked his own personal safety to ensure the safety of others. Morley wondered what Fogarty would have made of the platitudes. he'd probably have laughed and said 'accomplished, me bollocks,' and laughed that big, thick laugh he had. As he typed it, it struck Morley that this was not just another body story worth a few sterling quid. This was a man who'd been part of his life for the past few months. And now he was dead.
And so there'd be no more late night taps on the window, enigmatic phonecalls or conspiracy theories.
As he tapped the spacebar on the keyboard, Morley saw the drops drip onto it from the top of his nose and as he finished the tributes to Fogarty, he saved his work, sobbed and turned away from the screen.

A fortnight after the drowning, Morley found the remainder of the list of green vans that Fogarty had given him. He looked at it for a second and wondered if there really was some connection between the deaths and the vans, but then reckoned it was all just part of Fogarty's over-active imagination, so he scrunched it up and threw it across the room and into the bin, finally eradicating himself of grand ideas about journalism awards and big mass suicide stories.

* * * *

Nightmusic

The clouds came in over the mountains around Meiringen, the tiny Swiss town nestled in the Alpine valley between Interlaken and Brienz. It was going to be another stormy one, the locals said, and they were usually right. They knew that when the clouds came in that early and covered the tip of the Eiger that it was going to be a windy few days. You could see the urgency in the faces of the people as they made their way from the Migros supermarket at one end of the town, laden down with shopping bags, preparing for a stormy weekend. Across the street, the ladies in the shoe shop came out and took in the stalls of shoes, while the owner of the walking and climbing gear shop did likewise, clearing the streets before the wind arrived. Because when that wind arrived down the valley, it would blow all before it, but not in a dangerous way. The hikers and the climbers had come down on the last cable car of the day, and the last few tourists of the season were warned about walking near the Reichenbach Falls, the 300 feet falls which pour over the rocks high on the mountain over the town. At night, its roar dominates the place as hundreds of tonnes of water came out of the woods and over the side of the hill crashing onto the rocks below.

He'd been at the Reichenbach Falls earlier that afternoon, as he had been every week since he'd arrived in the town. It had been twenty years since he took up the battered copy of *The Final Problem* in the Galway library and read how Conan Doyle had described it when he picked it as the place to kill off Holmes.

'It is, indeed, a fearful place. The torrent, swollen by the melting snow, plunges into a tremendous abyss, from which the spray rolls up like the smoke from a burning house. The shaft into which the river hurls itself is an immense chasm, lined byglistening coal-black rock, and narrowing into a creaming, boiling pit of incalculable depth, which brims over and shoots the stream onward over its jagged lip. The long sweep of green water roaring forever down, and the thick flickering curtain of spray hissing forever upward, turn a man giddy with their constant whirl and clamour.'

Here Holmes had died, killed off because Conan Doyle's wife Louise had her illness aggravated during a trip here. So in order to get more attention, she demanded that her husband kill off Holmes in this spot. The spot where Moriarty had grabbed him and where both men fell to

Nightmusic

their death is marked by a large white star. The ledge is almost unreachable, certainly by any member of the public, but it is clearly visible from the viewing platform on the far side of the Falls. He chuckled to himself the first time he saw the Falls and wondered if his struggle with the Guard on Galway Bay had been a bit like that last battle between Moriarty and Holmes. After all, one was a lawman and the other an incredible criminal brain. He climbed up here every Thursday, on his free day from his job on the Lake Thun ferry, and he'd sit and stare at the spot where the world's greatest lawman was dragged to his watery grave. But Holmes was only dead for a while, of course. Holmes was soon restored to life by public opinion, but for Malachy, Holmes had died forever that day in Meiringen in 1891.

But now with the storms approaching, he sat in the Steinhach Tea Rooms on the main street, watching the drama of the forthcoming storm unfold before him. He loved days like this, when the weather outside was threatening and the only place to be was indoors with a good book and a pot of hot tea.
'Ich mochte noch tee, bitte,' he said to the waitress as she passed by. She smiled and nodded, knowing that his German was not local, but knowing what he meant all the same.
She'd seen him in here before, the man with a piece of his ear missing and his bundle of books. He never said much, just drank his tea and took slow forkfuls of his meringue. He always tipped her because she gave him extra scoops. The meringue was invented here. He'd read that in one of the Holmes brochures the Society had been sending him, hence the name of the town. And it was divine, filled with ice-cream and fresh cream and bulging over the side of the dish. He knew that Mother would never approve of him eating so many sweet things, but she wasn't around to bother him anymore. She had God to nag now.

To get to his house, he had to walk through the main street of the town and past the bronze statue of Holmes by John Doubleday. The statue contains clues to each of the Holmes stories and members of the Society come here on one of their trips and see if they can spot them all. Just in from this there is a complete replica of Holmes' apartment at 221B Baker Street built in a former English church opened in 1991 on the anniversary of Holmes death at Reichenbach Falls. Even the Square outside is known as Conan Doyle Place and up the street there is a hotel

Nightmusic

named after Sherlock. He knew about this place from the brochures, but this was even better than a fact-finding trip. Now he was a resident and had a place and town of his own.

He hadn't been able to send flowers to Mother's funeral as he'd been in transit then, but he sent a bouquet to her grave some months later. He wanted to write 'With Love from Wolfgang' on it, but he realised he couldn't take chances like that, so they went cardless.

In Switzerland, he didn't have to do any hunting. No more putting his neck on the line to get girls. No more wondering if he would slip up and be caught. No more having to listen to screams and see tear-filled eyes behind the tape. Now for the first time he could live as a normal person. A second chance. Like Holmes, he'd been brought back to life.

Here he wasn't the only Wolfgang in town. There was one he'd met at the small clean Catholic church at the end of the town and another at a music recital. He spoke music to them both and he spoke Holmes to them and they didn't look at him strangely like those in the music shop did years ago or at the concert in UCG. But here in Meiringen, they spoke about music and literature from the heart and not from a college book.

Every so often he would take the train into Lucerne and stock up on English books from the many fine bookstores in the town, or replace his Mozart collection with something from the music stores of Basle. And he'd let the music float through the walls of the cottage he rented on the Interlaken road.

Sometimes, he thought of Shantalla and of how he could never go back there, and of how eventually his body would not surface from the bay and people would get suspicious and begin to ask questions. He was pleased with the way he had anonymously rang the gardai when he swam ashore to tell them he saw the accident on the boat and to make it clear he was in the water. He was clever like that, but perhaps a bit too clever. Sometimes he wished he had just been ordinary and not messed around with like he was. Sometimes he wanted to kill them all. Father Curtin and the ones he had killed. Killing them once was never enough to release the anger and anyway once they were dead they were free of it all, unlike himself. He'd lost count of how many had been brought to the cellar on the farm. Twenty, thirty or forty, at least.

Nightmusic

He couldn't tell. Many of them had gone home again, but many hadn't. And many more had died elsewhere just to cover up the fact that so many young people were jumping into the river.

He took another spoon of meringue, the silver spoon crashing into its surface like an Arctic icebreaker, and sending powdery fragments onto the table. The first clap of thunder sounded over the town and the clouds moved in low, shielding the Reichenbach Falls from the town and enveloping Meiringen in a sea of grey. Then the heavens opened. Other people in the Tea Rooms moved over to the window to see the lightning strikes away to the East illuminating the only bit of the Eiger that was visible.
The tea arrived and the waitress smiled.
She left the pot down on the table and wiped away the crumbs.
'Danke,' he said
She was pretty, with brown eyes, and shoulder length brown hair tied back with a clip.
She smiled again and he looked at her and thought of what she would look like with some tape around her face and her legs strapped to a table.
Then he shut his eyes and thought of what Holmes said.
'It's a wicked world Watson, and when a clever man turns his brain to crime it is the worst of all.'

The End